WHEN CHRISTMAS COMES HOME FROM THE WAR

Bob Whiddon, Jr.

Published by

Bob Whiddon, Jr.
Me Third Publications
503-313-0623
dr_whiddon@msn.com

God First, Others Second, Me Third.

ISBN: 978-1-7344771-1-5

Cover Design by JKP

Back cover photo taken by Stephanie Steward.

To my wife, Debbie
Who has been with me all these years
In sickness and in health
For richer for poorer
And in all of the good and bad times in life
I love you forever

TABLE OF CONTENTS

FINDING THE PERFECT SANTA

Heather Smith had been working for Channel 21 News in Denver for almost five years. She was mostly an on-the-scene reporter covering breaking news or special stories. She would anchor a newscast when the regulars were on vacation or on assignment. But for at least five years she had been waiting for her big break.

Her boss was Randy Smith, no relation, with whom she got along with OK. Nothing special but not a close partnership. She dreaded when he would send her out on a fluff piece or some remote story that would take her the better part of the day to complete. Today would be no different. She was about to get a story that would change her life. But she would just view it, at first, as another story that was below her paygrade and below her intelligence.

"Heather," he barked, "come into my office. I have an assignment for you."

She picked up her pad and pen, rolled her eyes away from his sight, and walked to his office. It was a mess, as usual. Papers all over the place. Piles of old stories, possible stories, and glory stories that got the station a bit of recognition.

"Pack your bags. I'm sending you to Oklahoma," he said stoically.

"Oklahoma?" she asked. "What's in Oklahoma that could possibly be of interest to our Denver viewers? And, aren't there news stations there? Why do I have to go?"

"Save your complaining," said her boss. "I'm sending you to cover a story that other people have tried to cover. But no one has been successful in finding the real story." He paused for a moment to look at her sour disposition. "There is a report that there is a perfect Santa who appears every year then disappears. No one has been able to get the real story. They report on how great he is and how much joy he spreads. But no one knows why he disappears after Christmas. And no one knows why he just appears at the exact same time the next year."

"Oh, Brother! Why me?" she asked.

"It's because you have a knack in getting to the bottom of a story," he explained. "You can sniff out the truth. Like the Fosterman story. And, you may have to be there for a couple of weeks. And, I know you don't have any family around here to spend Thanksgiving with."

The Fosterman story helped launch Heather into notoriety in the Denver market. There was this woman who was being evicted from her rent house. Mrs. Fosterman told people she paid her rent every month. But it didn't help her any that she was loud, obnoxious, and violent to the landlord, even the police, who tried to kick her out. When Heather arrived she got Mrs. Fosterman to settle down. She said that she paid her rent each month with a money order she purchased from the local drug store. But she didn't have any receipts. It was easy for Heather to hunt down the paper trail of money orders to the landlord. But what she found out as she was investigating the story is that Michael Johnson, a District #3 councilman, was trying to purchase the property where Mrs. Fosterman was renting her house. A big box store wanted the land for new construction. He was putting pressure on the landlord to evict Mrs. Fosterman and free up the property. When Heather broke the story, the councilman resigned and the landlord was fined by the city.

"But if this is a Christmas story, why do I have to go before Thanksgiving?" she asked. "How long am I supposed to be in Oklahoma?"

The boss replied, "You may have to be there until the perfect Santa comes out of his shell. Should be on December 11th. You can do all the prep work, interviews and such, and be ready when he bursts on the Christmas scene."

"Well, that'll be two weeks," she complained, "no, three weeks. Can't you send someone else?"

"No. You are the only one who might be able to break this story," he said. "No one else has been able to do it. Good luck. Send me a postcard from Oklahoma."

Heather was irate. She fumed, but under her breath. Before she left the office that day she did some surfing of the Internet. There he was—the perfect Santa. He arrives on scene on December 11th every year and disappears after Christmas. "Well, here's something interesting. He's a local war hero. Maybe that's the angle."

She made all the arrangements, received her travel vouchers, rental car voucher, and per diem vouchers, then flew from Denver to Tulsa. Her destination was Blackwater, Oklahoma, a town with a population of about 20,000 just south of Tulsa. She thought she might have to stay in Tulsa and drive out every day. But when she arrived in Blackwater she found it to be a nice little town with a few good hotels. She checked into the local Holiday Inn Express since it had a café next door.

She took her luggage to her room and decided to unpack her stuff later. Because she had missed lunch, she went to the café for some dinner. It was a nice café, good food with a good atmosphere. When she was almost done with her dinner, the waitress came by to ask if she needed anything else.

"Well, I'm wondering, Tina" she said as she noticed the name on the name tag, "if you could help me find someone. I'm looking for a man named Tony Sanders. He's supposed to be…"

"…the perfect Santa," Tina interrupted as she completed Heather's sentence. "Everyone loves him. He is the reason we have such a great Christmas season. People come from miles just to see him and have their kids sit on his lap. He has more energy than any Santa I've ever seen. He has put Blackwater on the map!"

"Then people say he disappears every year right after Christmas," Heather continued.

"Yep. He's kind of a recluse," Tina said. "Not much into conversation during the rest of the year. They say he's a war hero, Viet Nam. That was before my time. But the museum has some of his stuff. There's some medals they gave him after the war, there's some news stories, and pictures and such. You ought to go over there tomorrow when it's open. Anything else you need, Ma'am?"

"Just one more thing," she began. "Do you happen to know where I might find Tony Sanders, the perfect Santa."

"Oh sure," said Tina with a small bit of excitement. "He's right over there." She pointed to a booth on the other side of the café. He was an older man. He had the white hair and the white beard. But he didn't look much like old St. Nick. He sported a Denver Bronco cap. He was wearing a tattered old coat and a scarf that didn't match either the cap or the coat.

"I thought you said he was a recluse?" Heather asked to get come clarification.

"Oh, he is," she said. "He's here almost every day at dinner time. He's nice, but doesn't want to say much."

Heather thanked the waitress as she paid her bill for dinner, along with a generous tip. She got up from her table and walked towards the perfect Santa who was, in her estimation, from what she saw, a great exaggeration. He didn't look perfect in anyway and there was no joy exuding from his appearance.

As she walked towards the occupied booth Tony noticed her then turned quickly away. When she got a little closer to his booth, Tony said, "What do you want?" His voice was gruff and his tone showed that he was slightly irritated with this visitor who came to ruin his quiet dinner time.

"Hi, Mr. Sanders, I'm Heather Smith. I'm a reporter...," she tried to explain but was interrupted.

"I don't like reporters. I don't like talking to reporters." Tony Sanders was clear and terse. And he didn't lift up his eyes to meet hers. He just wanted her to go away. But he knew she wouldn't. He knew that reporters had to keep bugging people until they got what they wanted.

Heather tried again, with a soft voice, to convince him that she was different from other reporters. "I would like to ask permission to sit and talk with you sometime, not necessarily tonight, but sometime. I'm from Denver and news of your Christmas work has reached us in Colorado."

Tony sighed, well it was more of a huff. "I guess I can't get you to go away." He took another bite of his dinner. "If you want to ask me a couple of questions, go ahead."

Heather said "Thank you" as she sat down in the booth across from Tony. "People say you are a recluse. Does that mean you have no family around here?"

"Family?" he said with a small chuckle. "I got a huge family. A good wife, children, grandchildren, a couple of greats. There all over the place."

"So you're married?" she asked wondering if he was a widower.

"Yep. Married. About 48 years now." There was a small grin emerging from Tony's beard covered face. "Beautiful woman. High School sweetheart."

Perplexed as to why he was eating in the café alone, she asked, "Is she out of town? Is that why you're here at the café all by yourself?"

"No. Can't stand her cooking." Heather just sat with a puzzled look on her face. Tony sighed, or huffed again and said, "Breakfast and lunch are OK. But for dinner she likes to experiment and try new things." He paused to take another bite of his meal.

"Can't stand new things. I just want hamburgers or plain food like this chicken-fried chicken. Don't like beans or vegetables or anything with cooked fruit. She invites friends or family over for dinner. I come here to eat something good. And I like being alone."

Tony spoke well, in Heather's estimation. He was articulate but abrupt. Still trying to get a read on him, she asked, "Why do you become the perfect Santa every year at the same time?"

"Because it's Christmas! It would be stupid of me to do it at Thanksgiving or Valentine's Day." Tony had a bit more irritation in his voice at this point.

"I'm sorry to be so nosey," she said, "but that's what I really want to know about you. I mean, you're here out in public. Everyone knows who you are. And frankly you don't come off as a jolly old soul. So, why all of a sudden on…," Heather looked at her notes, "on December 11th you automatically turn in the world's greatest Santa Claus?"

Tony kept silent for a few moments. He took a couple more bites of his dinner and pushed his plate aside. After wiping his mouth and beard, he cleared his throat and said in an almost whispered voice, "It's my penance."

Heather leaned closer and said, "I'm sorry. I didn't hear you."

"It's my penance," Tony said in a raised voice which he immediately lowered. He looked around the café to make sure than no one heard what he said. Then leaning in towards Heather he continued. "It is my penance for stuff that I did a long time ago. I figure if I make people happy at Christmas time then maybe that will erase some of that old stuff."

Looking a bit confused, Heather asked, "So you turn on the Santa stuff December 11th and turn it off again after December 25th? What about the rest of the year?"

"I can't be Santa all year long. That would be stupid!" As Tony said this he started to turn in the booth as if he was ready to leave.

"Can I ask just a couple more questions?" Tony nodded hesitatingly. "You said the Santa stuff was penance for stuff you did a long time ago." She paused to look deep into his eyes. Then softly she asked, "Did this have anything to do with the war?"

She looked deep into his eyes because she wanted to see if there would be any reaction to taking this man back almost 50 years to a dark time in American history. She saw that his eyes were tearing up a little.

Tony took out a tissue from his coat pocket and wiped his eyes and nose. "Stupid allergies" he said trying to cover over the fact that he was tearing up. He sighed, or huffed again, and said, "You seem like a nice woman. And I appreciate you trying to be gentle with your questions and your digging into my past. And you'll eventually find everything you need. But I don't like talking about the stuff that happened."

He sat for a moment thinking. His head was down, looking at the floor. "I suppose, if you want to hear about the stuff, you can come to my appointment tomorrow. My counselor, at the VA, makes me retell the…stuff…every time I see him. He thinks it will help me accept it and go on with my life." He paused to again wipe tears from his eyes. "I'll get him to let you observe the session. That way you can hear the story and I won't have to repeat it to you personally. How would that work?"

She thought for a moment. Then said to herself, "VA? Counselor? It does have something to with the war." Then aloud to Tony, she asked, "Will the counselor let me be in on your session?"

"Yah. It's been done before," he said. "Lots of reporters over the years have asked me about the stuff. The counselor thinks it helps if others hear about the stuff. I don't think so. But as long as Uncle Sam is paying the counselor, I have no problem talking."

Tony told her where the Veterans Administration offices were in Blackwater. He said his appointment was at 2:00pm. Then he gave her a slight warning of what to expect.

"When you hear my story, well, you might not sleep so good that night," he explained. "And don't get any ideas on how to help me. The VA has tried for years to help me forget what happened and they have not succeeded. But I'm OK just living my life as it is. Neither you nor anyone else can erase what I saw."

With that, Tony stood up, grabbed his cane that was sitting in the booth beside him, and limped away to the door. He walked away into the darkness.

Heather stood there wondering what had just happened and what to do next. She had been invited to attend a counseling session at the VA and listen as a Viet Nam veteran retells his story. And she would not be the first to experience such a privilege. And, when he warned her not to try to help him, well she just took that as a challenge.

Heather had done a report on PTSD (Post-Traumatic Stress Disorder) a couple of years before coming to Blackwater, Oklahoma. She had an idea of what was going on inside of a veteran who witnessed the horrors of war. She also had some ideas on the kinds of therapies that worked well with those veterans. She had her work cut out for her. But she was not discouraged. She enjoyed challenges. Maybe that's why she was sent to interview the perfect Santa. Maybe she would be the one to finally break the real story and help this wounded veteran come to terms with the horror.

Heather went back to the hotel. Before going to sleep she opened up her laptop and searched for news stories from the Viet Nam war, the stories that specifically named Tony Sanders. She was able to find out many things about him. He was not a soldier; he was a chaplain. He was a minister who was drafted into the army to help support soldiers in war. He held the rank of Second Lieutenant. The Chief of Chaplains assigned him to Bravo Company which was based near the DMZ (De-Militarized Zone). He was wounded while out on patrol.

"Out on patrol?" Heather wondered. "Why would they send a chaplain out on patrol during a war?"

The article went on to say that he was honored for bravery because he helped rescue five soldiers from enemy forces. "An army chaplain, out on patrol, and he helped rescue soldiers from the enemy?" she thought. The more she read the more questions she came up with to ask Tony the next time they were able to visit.

The article said Second Lieutenant Anthony Sanders was awarded the Purple Heart for being wounded in action. And he received the Medal of Honor for bravery in rescuing soldiers. "Wow," she said to herself. "This is not just the perfect Santa, he's the perfect hero." But those thoughts quickly faded as she remembered the broken man she talked with at the café.

She wrote down all of the questions that came to mind on a tablet. There were so many questions that it took up three sheets of paper. And there would be more when she could talk to Tony face to face. She clicked over to her email and composed a quick letter to her boss.

"Hi, Randy. Just wanted to update you on my first half day here in Blackwater, Oklahoma. I actually met the perfect Santa at the café tonight. He doesn't look the part of the Santa Claus. But he has a remarkable back story. He is a true war hero, swimming in PTSD. And no one in the past forty plus years has been able to really help him work through it. It's like he's stuck in the past and cannot get out. I, of course, take this as a challenge. I'll keep you informed. And, thanks for the assignment."

With that email sent, Heather settled down for a good night's sleep. She was excited about the possibilities of the story. Almost too excited. It took her a while to fall asleep. But she did. The real work begins tomorrow.

WHAT OTHERS SAID ABOUT
THE PERFECT SANTA

The next morning Heather tried to get an early start. But when she found out that the museum didn't open until 9:00am she decided she had time to eat some breakfast. At the café she took the same booth she had the night before. Tina the waitress was there also.

"Well, hi there, stranger," Tina said with a bubbly voice.

"Oh please, call me Heather. I think I'm going to be in your town for a while." As the waitress poured the first cup of coffee, Heather asked, "Do you have time to talk with me about Tony Sanders? I'm a reporter from Channel 21 in Denver and my boss sent me here to find the real story behind the perfect

Santa Claus. He said many have tried but no one has given him answers that he is satisfied with."

"Oh sure," Tina responded with a lilt in her voice. "But this is the breakfast rush and I can't talk now. If you come back at about ten o-clock I can talk while I take my break."

After making an appointment to return at 10:00 sharp, Heather took her time in consuming her delicious breakfast. When she was done she asked Tina for directions to the local museum. It wasn't far, so Heather decided to walk the distance and enjoy the fresh morning air.

The county museum was housed in a very old building. The corner of the building said that it was built in 1896. Inscribed in stone was a sign that indicated the building was originally the Henderson County School. Underneath the stone sign was a more modern sign on porcelain that read Henderson County Museum. Admission was free but they did take donations. Heather entered the building and inhaled the musty air of a 120-year old structure. It was not a disgusting aroma. To her it smelled like rich history. She pulled out a $10 bill and placed it into the donation box at the front desk. As she began her walk around the building she acted like a little girl who saw Disneyland for the first time.

As she viewed the various displays near the door she soon realized that she was in the middle of the Chickasaw Nation. The artwork, the rugs, the pottery, the pictures, the maps, she was amazed at the native American history and traditions. She then spotted the display honoring Second Lieutenant Anthony R. Sanders.

The first thing she saw was a large picture of Tony, a very young Tony, with his military uniform on. The caption read 1968 Graduate of US Army Chaplain's School. There was a full-page newspaper article about him being sent to Viet Nam. The picture in the newspaper article showed him wearing fatigues and a helmet. Underneath the newspaper page hung two medals: the Purple Heart, awarded to soldiers wounded in battle, and the Medal of Honor, awarded to him for bravery in rescuing five soldiers from enemy combatants. There was another newspaper clipping with a picture next to the Medal of Honor. It was Tony receiving the Medal of Honor from then

President Nixon. The date read January 5, 1970. Underneath that picture was another article, also cut out of a newspaper, with a picture of Tony and nine other men as they walked back onto their base. The headline of the story read "Army Chaplain leads ambush to rescue captured US soldiers."

Heather stood and stared at that last picture for several minutes. It was not the best of quality, like it had been taken with an old Polaroid Camera. He was bandaged on his left hip and leg. But what caught her eye was Tony's face. He was helping another soldier walk who was also heavily bandaged. But it was the look on Tony's face that caught her eye. It was a look of utter hopelessness. It didn't make sense to her. He was a hero. He led those soldiers back to the safety of the base. He should have had relief all over his face. But in the midst of cheers and excitement, Tony looked hopelessly lost. "That's the same hopeless-ness I saw on his face last night," she said to herself.

Heather tried to imagine how a chaplain got involved in an ambush of enemy soldiers and how he was successful in rescuing nine American soldiers. She was not alive during the Viet Nam war, but she learned about it in history classes and by reading stories in books and newspapers. How could a chaplain, a minister, become such a war hero?

"Good morning, Miss," a gentle voice sounded, but it shattered Heather's concentration. "Are your finding what you're looking for?"

It was the front desk attendant for the museum. Heather was a bit surprised. When she calmed down she said, "Yes, thank you. I came to see the display about Tony Sanders. Is this all there is about Tony in the museum. Seems a rather small display for such a great war hero."

"Oh, I agree," replied the attendant, "but this is all that little Tony would allow us to display."

"Little Tony?" Heather asked, hoping to understand the "little" adjective.

"Oh yes, I knew Tony as a little boy. I'm about ten-years older than he. I used to babysit him from time to time." The attendant thought for a moment. "He was really a happy boy, full of energy. I am proud of what he did in the war. And I sure am glad he survived. But when he came back home, he seemed…lost."

Heather had a confused look on her face. It was intentional, hoping to get more clarification. "But people say that at Christmas time he becomes the perfect Santa, full of joy and hope and spreading as much happiness as he possibly can. Then he just goes back into hiding."

"Folks around here stopped trying to figure that out a long time ago," the attendant admitted. "We just enjoy the perfect Santa no matter how short a time we get to see him."

Heather had many more questions. A small group of school children arrived at the front door to the museum. The attendant excused herself and went off to help the children.

"Curiouser and curiouser," she thought to herself as she remembered that famous line from Alice in Wonderland. She looked at her watch and saw it was getting close to 10:00am. She took out her cell phone and took a picture of the display honoring Tony. Then she left the museum and walked back to the café.

By the time she got back to the café Tina, the waitress, was already in a booth eating her breakfast.

"Hi, stranger, come on over," she said in her bubbly voice.

"I hope this is a good time for you to answer some questions," Heather began. "I don't want to take away from your free time."

"Oh, no worries," Tina said. "I can answer all the questions you have, at least for the next half hour."

"I want to know more about this perfect Santa act that Tony puts on," she said. "What makes it so perfect?"

"Well first of all, it's no act," Tina objected with a smile. "He is the real thing. You should see his Santa suit. It's the best one I've ever seen. And the kids, oh how he loves the kids. He calls them all by their first name. He remembers all of them! And if he meets a new kid, the next year he remembers that name, too. The parents love him. Even when a child asks for something extravagant, he always seems to know how to turn that around, to get the child to do something special for his parents or some neighbor. And when he's not on his Santa chair he's walking around town spreading cheer. If he sees someone lugging groceries, he stops to help. If someone is putting up Christmas lights, he stops to help. He has an endless supply of energy and joy."

"So, it all begins on December 11th?" Heather asked.

"Yep, like clockwork," Tina answered.

"Then he just stops it all on December 26th?" Heather again asked.

"Yep, that's the thing. On the 11th a Christmas light just turns on and then it turns off on the 26th." Tina wrinkled her brow to look puzzled. "Then he just goes back to being a loner, like the man you saw last night. I wish he was happy the rest of the year."

Heather paused to try to pose the next question as gently as possible. "Some heard him say that the perfect Santa activities are his penance. Have you heard that? Do you know what he might be talking about?"

"Well, I've talked with this family, you know, his wife, and his children come to the café every-once-in-a-while. What I gather from listening to them is that something horrible happened during the war. Something that he's not proud of. And even though he saved some soldiers, there's some secret that he's hanging on to." Tina stopped to wipe a tear from her eye. "He's a good man. I just pray that all the doctors he goes to will figure out what to do for him to bring him out of his nightmare. It's been a long nightmare."

"Tina, I need you," hollered the café manager.

"Be right there," Tina responded. "I'm sorry, I have to get back to work. I hope I helped you some."

"You were a great help," Heather said. She got Tina to tell her where Tony lived before she clocked back in.

Heather wanted to see where Tony lived. She was curious about what kind of lifestyle he had. His house was on the other side of the small town and she assumed it was too far for her to walk. She drove her rental car this time.

The neighborhood where he lived was older but well kept. His house was an older house with a covered front porch. When Heather pulled up she noticed an older woman sitting on the porch swing. It could have been Tony's wife but she wasn't sure.

She parked the car at the curb and got out. The older woman met her half way up the walk.

"You must be the reporter from Denver," the woman said. "I'm Georgia, Tony's wife. He told me a good looking younger woman was asking him questions at the café. Welcome to our home."

"Well thank you so much. I'm Heather Smith from Channel 21 News in Denver," Heather said. "I am honored to be here and to meet you. I have an appointment with Tony at his VA counselor's office this afternoon. He said I could be there to observe his session."

"Oh, of course. He has done that before," said Georgia. "His counselor makes him retell 'the story' at each session. He hopes that something will click sometime and help him out of his fog. So far it hasn't worked. But we're still hoping and praying."

By this time Georgia had escorted Heather into her kitchen and had her sit at the table. After pouring her some hot tea, she sat down with her and said, "What would you like to know?"

Heather opened up the notebook that she used to write down notes. She said, "I assume that you know the story of what happened during the war."

"Yes," she answered, "but you need to hear it from him. He has no problem talking about it, at least in counseling. But I have to warn you, it's not a pretty story. But it was war. Nothing is pretty in war."

"Then maybe you can tell me a little about Tony, the man," said Heather. "How did you meet? What were your hopes and dreams? Tell me about your family. What kind of man was he before the war? And how was he different when he came home? Wow. I really unloaded on you. Start wherever you like."

Georgia took a deep breath. And with a smile on her face she began. "Tony was a wonderful young man. We were High School sweethearts. After High School I went off to Oklahoma State University and he went off to Oklahoma Christian University. We kept our romance alive through phone calls, letters, and weekend visits. After he graduated, he went off to Trinity Seminary and got his master's degree in theology. We were married in May of 1966 right after his graduation. His first ministry position was right here in Blackwater. And he loved it. We had two kids right away. And a third was on the way when he was 'requested' by Uncle Sam to be an Army Chaplain. He was kind of discouraged, but kind of excited about helping out soldiers who could use lots of encouragement during the war."

Georgia had to stop for a moment as she began to tear up. "All I could think about is that he would go off to war, get killed, and never see his baby. I know that's kind of selfish. But that's how I felt. He said he would be gone for only two years. But that didn't help."

She got up to get the tea kettle to refill the tea cups. "He went off to Chaplain's training school and graduated as a Second Lieutenant. He was very proud. I was very proud. And he went off to war." She had to wipe more tears. "Came back one year later. And everything was different."

"Different?" asked Heather. "How was he different?"

"Well, he was happy to see us. He gave me a big kiss. He hugged our kids, and cradled our newborn." She paused again, like she was trying to think of what to say next. "We had a wild passionate night. That's why we now have four kids." She giggled. "And he tried to go back to the church to work and serve and preach. But it was a real struggle for him. It took him a while, but he finally told me 'the story' about what happened." She sighed. "They flew him to Washington DC so President Nixon could give him the Medal of Honor. When he came back, he wasn't happy. He put the medal in his sock drawer. He sank into a depression. He started going to counseling, but it didn't seem to help. He started having no patience with me or the kids. About ten years after he came home he made the decision to sleep in the apartment above the garage." She cried as she recalled that night.

Heather touched her arm in an attempt to console her. "Take your time."

Georgia continued. "He was still a great man. He was gentle to me. When he felt that things were too much for him to handle, he politely left the room. Our children still had a gentle dad. He went to all their events and games. He watched them graduate from High School and college. He attended their weddings. And he was so happy to see grandkids come along. Family was still important to him. And I was still important, too. He tried, but he just couldn't handle much of his daily life. A part of him died in Viet Nam."

Heather wrote down some last notes. Then she closed her notebook. It was time for her to stop the interview. "Thank you for sharing with me. I see how this is wearing you out."

"No, no," she interrupted, "I'm fine. Uncle Sam pays for him to tell his story on a regular basis. I don't get to tell my story very often. I appreciate you listening to me unload on you."

The two women stood and embraced. A new friendship had been created. "I'll come back again and you can tell me exactly what you told me before. The more you tell your story the closer you come to accepting it."

Heather left Tony's house feeling she had a good understanding about Tony and his home life. She also felt sorrow that Georgia was wrestling with "the story" that he brought back with him from Viet

Nam. But she also had a new determination to figure out something that might help this wonderful couple, this wonderful family. She looked at her watch and saw that it was time to be at Tony's counseling session.

As she was driving towards the VA, she started making a mental evaluation of what she learned about Tony so far. First he was a wonderful man, husband, and father before he went off to war. Then the ugly thing happened in the war and he came back changed. But, there were still glimpses of the wonderful man he was before he left. And, he recognized when he was being not so nice to his wife and family. So he would distance himself from them, for a while. But he still tried, really hard, to continue to be the man, husband, father, and now grandfather that his family needed. So, she thought, he's still in there. It's like there's a curtain hanging in the middle of his life. It's like it was shielding him from becoming ugly before his family. And that's good, sort of. But the curtain is also keeping those he loves away from the man who was changed because of the ugly event of the war.

Her logic was well developed. Is the solution then to get more of the people he loves so dear to enter into his ugly war life to understand where he is coming from? Or, is the solution to bring more of his war life into the lives of the people he loves so much? Then she felt a bit foolish. If trained psychologists haven't been able to figure out how to help Tony for almost fifty years after the war ended, how will a news reporter ever be able to figure how to help a soldier experiencing PTSD? She decided to stop trying to think of solutions for now. But Heather would later look back on this moment. She doesn't see it now, but she'll look back and see that today was the day she started growing in wisdom and compassion for the wounded soldiers that come home. And that a seed of a solution had been planted in her mind.

"THE STORY"
BEHIND THE PERFECT SANTA

Heather arrived at the VA office building at 1:45pm for Tony's appointment. She checked in with the receptionist who gave her a set of forms to fill out. The forms included confidentiality and non-disclosure language. She told the receptionist, "I was invited to sit in on Tony Sander's counseling session. I am a reporter and he knows that I will use what I hear in my story."

The receptionist smiled as she explained. "Yes, we've had reporters here before. Mr. Sanders and the doctor will tell you what you can and can't disclose. And these forms say that you will abide by what they say."

It made sense to her. She signed the forms and gave them back to the receptionist.

Tony entered the VA offices a little before 2:00pm. He and Heather exchanged pleasantries. When Tony was called back for his session the receptionist asked her to stay in the waiting room for a little while. "Mr. Sanders will go through a health check and routine questions before they call you in."

It was only a matter of about ten minutes before Heather was allowed to enter the counseling office. Tony said, "Heather, this is Dr. Billings. He's my shrink. This is Heather Smith a reporter from Denver."

After shaking hands and exchanging hellos, Dr. Billings explained to Heather the ground rules for her presence in Tony's session. "Miss Smith, this is a counseling session governed by HIPAA rules. In general, nothing that is said here is supposed to leave this office. However, over the years Mr. Sanders has allowed reporters in to hear his story. So, with his permission you may use anything you hear in your news story. But there is one caveat. If there is any new information or any new breakthrough that happens today, I will advise Mr. Sanders to require those new details to remain confidential. It will be his choice and I expect you to abide by his decision. Agreed?"

Heather said, "Certainly. I agree."

With that the doctor asked some questions about how Tony felt and how the past week had gone. After about five minutes of these kinds of questions, the doctor asked if he was ready to tell his story.

"This is as good a time as any," Tony said.

Heather already had her notebook opened up. She shifted a little on her chair and got ready to write notes. Then Tony began.

"I was drafted to serve in the Army in 1968. I already had a master's degree and was an ordained minister. So they sent me to the Army Chaplains School. They taught me how to be an officer, how to perform rites and ceremonies of various religious groups. I wasn't going to serve just those who believed like I do. It was OK. Kind of eye opening. But it went well and I graduated in November of 1968.

Right after Thanksgiving they shipped me off to Viet Nam. I eventually arrived at a base where I was processed and received my first assignment. I was embedded with Company B, Bravo Company. For the most part I stayed at the base and took care of the kids. Most of them were barely 18-years old. A few times they sent me out with them especially if they thought the mission might be dangerous. That didn't make me feel good. But the kids were well trained and we always came back.

"There were times when I was terrified every moment of every day. Then there were times when nothing happened and I was bored to tears. And the locals...? They didn't seem to appreciate us for being in their country. They walked around like they were lost. I didn't see any life in their eyes and couldn't find any hope in their hearts. We shared our chocolate bars and cookies with the children. It brightened up their lives for a while. Then they would disappear quickly. I learned that they knew when bad stuff was about to happen a whole lot sooner than we did.

"Then all Hell would break loose. Machine gun fire, bombs, sirens, yelling, screaming." Tony closed his eyes tightly as he told this part of the story. "After a while the noise would stop. But then the wounded would be brought in. Some carried between two soldiers. Some in trucks. Some on stretchers covered head to toe with a blanket. I saw dead soldiers every day. At first I cried miserably. Then the tears stopped flowing. It was just war. It was just what happened in war. There was nothing I could do."

Tony had to stop for a few minutes. He wiped the tears from his eyes. He took some deep breaths. Heather looked at the doctor. He motioned to her as if this was just part of the process. Tony regained his composure and began again.

"My first Christmas in Viet Nam, well, my only Christmas in Viet Nam was surreal. It was December in 1969 and soldiers started talking about Christmas at home. They told about traditions as well as unique things that their families did at the holidays. But every one of them ended their stories the same way. Their countenance faded into gloom.

Their eyes became very sad. Then they just stopped talking. The war was very good at replacing hope with hopelessness.

"My job as a chaplain was to try and make Christmas a bright spot in the middle of the huge black hole we were in. It was hard for me. Any hope I had was already replaced by hopelessness. But I did my best. Deep inside I knew it wouldn't help much. But the kids deserved my honest effort. So I planned. We were supposed to have turkey brought in for them. I planned a Christmas sermon. I cried a lot. I waited for Christmas to come, and then go.

"On December 10, 1969, my patrol was sent out on a recon mission. They said that a small village had been destroyed by enemy fire. We were supposed to go assess the damage and see if there were any survivors. We walked several miles before we came to the village. It was bad. Everything destroyed. Bodies lay all over the place. Women and children. The children…"

Tony started crying. The doctor leaned over and touched his arm. "Take your time." It took a few minutes for the tears to stop. He wiped his eyes, blew his nose, cleared his throat and continued.

"Then, all Hell broke loose. It wasn't like the other times when it started off in the distance. Our patrol came under direct fire. Machine guns hit many of the kids. A bomb went off...maybe it was a grenade. I don't remember what happened right after that. I guess I was in a daze. Maybe unconscious for a while. When I woke up I had a searing pain on my left side. I had been hit by shrapnel. I looked around to see if I could find something to bandage my wounds. But what I saw were my kids, about a dozen of them, my buddies, lying dead. The others were not around. Maybe they went off after the enemy. I kept hearing gunfire. I couldn't tell if it was getting closer or farther away. I grabbed a gun from one the dead kids. And I didn't know where I was going but I had to find some help somewhere.

"I tried to remember the path that we had taken to get to that point. My mind wasn't thinking clearly. I did the best I could. I walked for about an hour and figured I was hopelessly lost. It was dark. I was in a jungle. I was scared.

"I heard noise in the brush ahead of me. I ducked down and waited to see who was there. My glasses were dirty and I couldn't see well. But to my surprise it was a patrol of four US soldiers. I didn't want to yell out for fear they would be startled and shoot. So I cried 'help me' in a medium loud voice. They asked if I was a friend or enemy. I said I was an American. We met face to face. They looked like all the other soldiers: young, dirty, scared, hopeless.

"There was a sergeant and three privates. They all called me sir. I forgot that I was an officer. The sergeant looked tough. He had been through war before. But he was still a kid. He introduced me to Curly, one of the privates. I said 'Curly?' He took off his helmet and showed me his curly red hair. The next private was Shorty. It was obvious how he got his nickname. The last private was Stewart. Kind of nerdy-looking kid.

"The sergeant told me that they had come under fire. His corporal and four other privates were captured by the enemy. He said that they had been wandering for about an hour trying to find help to rescue his men. He said 'Sir, you gotta help us.' A lot of things went through my mind, but a rescue mission was not one of them.

"I decided right then and there that I was going to die in the Viet Nam jungle that night. So I might as well try to help other soldiers. But I wasn't really a soldier. I was a minister, a chaplain. They only reason I was carrying a gun was because I was scared, deathly scared. I told the sergeant 'Let's go.' So we started walking towards where they last saw their buddies.

"We came across a small clearing in the jungle. On the other side we could see a campfire going. We sneaked up as far as we could and still feel comfortable with our distance. We could see the five US soldiers. They were tied up. The enemy soldiers were standing and laughing. None of us understood the language so we didn't know what they were saying. We couldn't rush them for fear they would shoot our buddies. An idea came to my mind."

Tony had to stop again. This was the moment. This is what was so awful that he has not been able to block it from his mind for almost fifty years. Again the doctor said, "Take your time." He took some deep breaths and began.

"I told the sergeant that each of us would pick an enemy soldier and shoot to kill. I wasn't a soldier, but I knew how to shoot a rifle. We agreed on which one of us would kill which one of the enemy soldiers. I said a little prayer for us, for our buddies, and for the enemy. Then I counted. One…two…three…."

Tony closed his eyes tightly as if he had heard the gunshot in the jungle. Then he began to cry uncontrollably.

"The rifles sounded together as if it was one shot. It echoed in the jungle night. Five enemy soldiers lay dead on the ground. I killed one of them. I killed one of them. I killed one of them. We went and untied our buddies. They grabbed rifles from the dead enemy soldiers and started to run. I just stood there. I stared at the kid I had just killed. He couldn't have even been 18-years old. He seemed a lot younger. But he was dead. I killed him.

"The sergeant came back and grabbed my arm. 'Come on, Sir, we need to go.' The sergeant knew where our base was. It seemed like it took hours to get there. A couple of the captured soldiers had been beaten severely by the enemy. I helped one of them walk. My left side hurt badly. But we needed to keep walking or we would be dead in the jungle that night.

"As we neared our base one of our sentries saw us and called to others to come and help us. I remember about twenty soldiers coming to help. I remember a flash going off. It must have been a camera. I remember that a medic treated by left hip and my left leg. After that I found my tent, went inside and cried all night long."

Tony was crying again. After a while the doctor said, "But you rescued five soldiers and you helped bring four more soldiers to safety. Ten of you walked out of the jungle that night."

Tony interrupted and screamed at the doctor. "But five people were killed that night! It was at my command that five people were killed that night! And I killed one of them! I CAN'T UN-SEE WHAT I SAW THAT NIGHT!"

Tony turned to Heather and screamed at her. "I CAN'T UN-SEE WHAT I SAW THAT NIGHT!"

Tony turned his body away from Heather and cried. She was also crying. She turned to the doctor to see what she should do. "Miss Smith, I think it's time you left the room. Anything you have heard here today, feel free to use in your story."

Heather stood. She wanted to run over and hug Tony. But she left the room.

When she got to her car she just sat there. Listening to such horror was fogging up her mind and her heart. The story was so vivid that it played in her mind over and over again. She put herself in Tony's shoes, imagining the jungle, the explosions, the fear, the shot, a young man falling dead as he watched down the barrel of a rifle. And the walk back to base with nine kids, in the dark, through a jungle that could have hidden other dangers.

She needed to get back to her hotel room so she could type Tony's story into her computer. She didn't know exactly what to do with the story but she had to write it all down while it was fresh in her mind. But then the story began to replay in her mind.

She cringed and shut her eyes tightly to stop the story. But she couldn't get it to stop. This was probably what Tony had been going through all of his life. She sat. Her eyes were closed. Tears ran down her face.

Knock, knock, knock. She was startled awake from her visions of the horrors of war. It was Tony knocking on her car window. "Are you OK in there?" he asked with concern.

"I'm OK," she lied. "I was just thinking about your story."

"Yeah, It'll keep you up some nights." Tony paused and thought for a moment. "Maybe we should go get a cup of coffee. You can tell me your story. I know how to be a good listener. I've had professional listeners for a lot of years."

"Yah, coffee might be good," she replied. Tony had walked to the VA. He lost his license years ago when his doctors believed he was a hazard to other drivers. Early, after the war, he would have nightmarish visions, sometimes during the day. He didn't mind that they took away his license to drive.

Blackwater, Oklahoma was a small enough town. He could get almost anywhere by walking.

Heather invited him to ride with her. They went off to the café next door to the hotel.

They sat down and ordered coffee. Heather took out her notebook, scanned a few pages, then put it down. "I'm not really sure I want to go back over your story right now." She thought for a moment. Then a light in her brain lit up. "You have said to me, and to others, that the things you do for everyone at Christmas time, as the perfect Santa, was your penance. Can you tell me about that, if it wouldn't be too painful for you to tell me?"

"I'm not sure I'm the perfect Santa," Tony said. He was embarrassed that people thought of him that way. To him he was just Santa for a few days in December. "The penance stuff is easy to talk about. December 10th is the date of that horrible story. I'm not much into socializing during the year. And even then I crawl into a deeper hole on December 10th and that night rushes over me. It's the darkest night of the year. Even my family knows not to try to find me or try to talk with me. It was Christmas time back then. Soldiers were talking about it, making plans to have some semblance of Christmas in the war zone. I was trying to promote the Christmas spirit. But that was all shot to hell. That's the Christmas I brought home from the war."

He teared up a little. Heather worried that he would come unglued as he did in his counseling session.

"So, I wake up on December 11th and think, 'What can I do to make Christmas a happy time?' I turn into Santa. I guess it's to make up for what was stolen from the soldiers that year, and what I stole from the enemy soldiers, too. Don't know if those people celebrate Christmas. But maybe they did, and maybe I stole it from them. Anyway, I don't want anyone to feel a fraction of the horror I felt that day. So, I spread cheer. I become Santa."

Heather was writing a few notes while he spoke. When she finished a lengthy note she looked at him and asked, "This Santa thing you do, is it real? Is it an act? Is it an annual routine where you go through the motions? What goes through your mind when you are Santa?"

Tony was quick to reply. He sported a big smile as he answered. "Oh, it's real. Even though I am trying to atone for what I did back in the war, I have so much fun. I love to see the faces of the people I help. I love to see little kids get all excited about Christmas. I love helping people with their chores, and shopping, and getting groceries to their cars. I love hanging decorations on storefronts. It's a great time of year. I feel good about life, like I did before the war. I feel good about myself like I used to feel. It's great."

By this time Tony was grinning from ear to ear. Just telling stories of how happy he could be helped him be happy in the moment. "Wow! That sounds like a wonderful time for you," Heather said. "Not to put a downer on this conversation, but then on December 26th you go back to being discouraged and depressed?"

"Well, not really," Tony replied as he looked like he was in deep thought. "The goodness and happiness lasts for a few days longer, maybe even a week. But I know the depression will hit soon so I crawl back into my hole and wait for it. When it does hit, I tell myself 'There it is! I knew it was coming.'"

Heather and Tony talked for another hour or so. It was mostly a pleasant conversation about family and friends, about Christmas and even Thanksgiving. The more he talked about the good things the more he smiled. And by the time Tony excused himself to go home the two had enjoyed a wonderful time over coffee at the café.

Heather went back to her hotel room and began writing her notes into the computer. Then a thought hit her. He gets happy when he talks about happy things. Maybe that's part of the solution to help him come to acceptance of the trauma he experienced in Viet Nam. But then she thought if this was a solution the doctors should have already thought of it. So she put it out of her mind, at least for now. She finished her typing and went to sleep. Tomorrow would be the day before Thanksgiving. She was going to have to find someplace to eat and celebrate the holiday, if that was at all possible.

POST-TRAUMATIC STRESS DISORDER, A SOLDIER'S WAR BAGGAGE

Heather got up late on that Wednesday, the day before Thanksgiving. She didn't sleep well. Just like Tony said. His war story kept her up, too. She figured that she finally fell asleep around 3:00am. When she woke up the ugly story of war was still racing through her brain.

She went to the café to get a small breakfast. Tina wasn't there. It was her day off. The other waitress explained that she volunteered to work on Thanksgiving Day so some other workers with families could spend the day at their homes. Heather found out that the café would be open all day Thanksgiving. It's for those who are alone and for the travelers. She qualified as both. The café would be her place for Thanksgiving dinner.

She took her rental car and drove around the town a bit to see what kinds of stores were open. Even in that small town every store was getting ready for Black Friday, the day after Thanksgiving when millions of shoppers began their rush to purchase Christmas gifts. She found a small grocery store and decided to go in and buy some snacks and bottled water. Her hotel room had a small kitchenette and a small refrigerator. And it looked like she was stuck in Blackwater for another couple of weeks. She needed to have the snacks for survival.

In the grocery story she ran across Georgia Sanders, Tony's wife. She was doing some last minute shopping for her Thanksgiving dinner.

"Well hi, Heather," said Georgia, bubbling over with so much happiness that she was about to explode. "It is good to see you again this morning."

"Hi, Georgia," she responded. "I'm here to get a few snacks for my hotel room."

"Well that's great," Georgia bubbled again. "What are you doing for Thanksgiving? Are you going back home? Do you have relatives close?"

"No. Denver is too far away just to run home for a day or two," she explained. "And I don't have any relatives in this part of the country. I've got a reservation at the café tomorrow to eat my dinner there."

"Oh, nonsense," interrupted Georgia. "You will have Thanksgiving dinner with us!"

"I don't want to be any bother," said Heather. "I don't want to mess up your family holiday."

"Oh, don't worry about that," Georgia insisted. "There's only a couple of family members coming tomorrow. You'll fit right in. You'll have a great time."

Heather was at a loss as to what to say or what kind of excuse she could possibly make up to get out of going to her house for the meal. She smiled at Georgia but didn't say anything.

"It's settled, then," said Georgia. "Come over around noon tomorrow. We may not eat till one o'clock or so. But you can help me with the final details of the feast. See you tomorrow." She sang that last line. Heather's estimation of Georgia—she's way too happy at Thanksgiving. She's probably way too happy all year long.

"Well, I guess I'm going to the Sanders' house for Thanksgiving. Yay." She didn't say this out loud. But even in her mind it had a slight tone of sarcasm.

As she was driving home she drove past the VA offices. Dr. Billings was standing outside, next to his car, talking to someone on his cell phone. As she neared, he hung up his phone and began to walk towards the door to his offices. Heather took the opportunity to see if he would be willing to talk a bit more about Tony.

"Hi, Dr. Billings," Heather called out. He stopped walking, recognized her, and turned back to talk with her.

"Hi, Miss Smith. What can I do for you?" said the doctor.

"I was wondering if you had time to talk with me about Tony just to help me understand him a little better?" Heather asked about possibly scheduling an appointment with him after the Thanksgiving break.

"Well I have time right now if you do," said the doctor. "I have no appointments the rest of the day. I came to the office to get caught up on some paperwork."

Heather gladly accepted the invitation to talk with him. When they arrived in his office the doctor reminder her about HIPAA rules of confidentiality. "Since you had permission to be in our counseling session yesterday I can answer any question about what was said. And if you want to ask general questions about soldiers and war, I can answer them, too. But if you wander into confidential matters about Tony, I cannot answer those questions."

"Agreed," she said. "Can I ask you about PTSD in general? I did a story on it for the news a couple of years ago. I thought I had a fair understanding of it and some of the therapies that are used with soldiers coming back from war. My assumption is that Tony has some degree of PTSD. But I am curious as to why he has come for counseling for a great number of years and yet he is still wrestling with his disorder. Is his diagnosis of PTSD more severe than other soldiers?"

The doctor cleared his throat and began to answer her. "PTSD by itself is a serious disorder for anyone who is diagnosed with it. I apologize if you already know what I'm about to tell you, but I need to start from the beginning. Any trauma that anyone experiences in life can throw them into some level of PTSD. It is more pronounced for soldiers because they see horrible things that most people will never see. And soldiers, especially, when they return do not find very many other people who could possible understand what they went through. They keep it inside, if festers, and it damages.

"Miss Smith, our brains are wonderful organs. They are designed to be wonderful. But when trauma happens, our brains are like cameras that film every aspect of the situation to be replayed at a later date. While we experience the trauma, our brains and the rest of our body comprehends the trauma in fast-motion. Heart rates increase, blood pressure sky rockets, we sweat profusely, and we panic, all in fast-motion. Then when the trauma passes, our brains replay the event in very slow motion. We start to see things that maybe we missed during the actual event. We're not making up new facts. We're just seeing the event in extremely great detail and in extremely slow motion. And just like the event itself, that we have trouble understanding or accepting, the replay makes it even harder to understand it or accept it. So, we spiral downward into depression. We re-live the event. It is still hard. We still do not accept it. We try to forget it. But we can't. We re-live it again. It is harder to see. It is harder to accept. It is harder to try to forget. So we go on. And re-run of the trauma replays daily, sometimes multiple times daily."

Heather remembered most of these details from her own research on the subject. She said, "I know that therapies for PTSD are not always successful, and when they are they are successful only after a great deal of time. Why is it taking so long for Tony to come to acceptance? Is there something special or weird or out-of-the-ordinary in his case?"

Dr. Billings thought for a moment, trying to decide if this questions fits in with the permission that Tony gave for her to hear his story. "Yes, with Tony there is something out-of-the-ordinary with his trauma. Tony was not trained as a soldier. He was trained as a minister. Soldiers are trained for combat. Ministers are trained to save lives, save souls, offer hope, offer salvation. So when this minister, dressed as a soldier, picked up a rifle and took a life instead of saving a life, two very different and opposite worlds collided. Even though in war it is 'permissible' to take the life of another human being, most normal people could never do it. So even normal soldiers come back unable to justify their own actions. Because Tony was trained, heavily trained, to save lives, he was not like the normal soldier who has problems with killing in war. For Tony the two worlds of human saving and human killing collided. And it was a violent collision."

Heather was taking notes as he talked. Then she asked, "Other than having him retell his story often, what kinds of therapies have you tried in his case."

"I'm sorry," said Dr. Billings. "That falls into

confidential matters that are not part of the permissions he gave to you earlier."

A fleeting thought entered her mind at that moment. She remembered that Tony said the joy and happiness he experienced while playing the Santa Claus did not abruptly go away on December 26th. He said it might last for a couple of days, maybe even a week. "Well, that's curious," she thought to herself. Then she asked, "Dr. Billings, do you know about how the Christmas spirit fades from Tony's life after Christmas?" She was a bit nervous about the questions since it was worded awkwardly. "He told me that it doesn't go away immediately on December 26th. It might even stay with him for a week or so."

"Tony has not talked to me about that," he said. "And I have not observed it myself. He always disappears from public on December 26th, like clockwork. He keeps his once-a-month appointments. But other than that, I don't see much of him."

Then she posed a hypothetical question. "Let's just say that there definitely is this Christmas spirit that hangs on for a week after Christmas. Do you have an idea on what might cause this Christmas 'hangover' so to speak?"

"Hmm," he began as he had to think about it. "I suppose that something like that could be attributed to Tony experiencing real happiness and real pride in what he does during Christmas. And it changes him, for a while, so the good feelings last for a while longer."

Dr. Billings thought for a moment. He continued, "I remember a study that was done in the 1980s that resulted in what we call the Mother-Teresa-Effect. A researcher was trying to measure the value of performing acts of service to people who could not repay the kindness. His idea was to show his students a video clip of Mother Teresa taking care of the poor people in Calcutta, India. They couldn't possibly pay her back. The researcher took saliva samples from his students before and after watching the video clip. He determined that the immune systems of his students were stronger after watching acts of service being done that they were before watching the video. Then he sent them out to perform acts of service. The same results were multiplied. They found that acts of kindness or acts of service, whether viewed or performed, actually cause a physiological change in people. That would make sense. That may be why Tony could continue having that good spirit even when Christmas season ends."

Their conversation went on for a few more minutes. Then Heather excused herself, thanked the doctor for his time, and went off to do more research into PTSD therapies.

Heather spent the rest of the night reading articles on the internet about PTSD. It all made sense to her. But to her, with an untrained mind in counseling and psychology, it seemed that most therapies are designed to rework the thought processes or change how a mind views a past event. They also deal with replacing ugly past events with more positive present and future events and activities.

On her way back to the hotel Heather stopped in at the café to get a bite to eat and to tell the staff that she would not be eating Thanksgiving dinner with them. "I was invited to eat dinner with Tony

Sanders and his family," she said somewhat sheepishly. "Georgia was very persuasive and I just couldn't tell her no."

The waitress understood what Heather was saying. She, too, had been bowled over by Georgia. It was hard to turn her down for anything.

Heather sat in her usual booth and ordered a sandwich and coffee. She was saving room for a slice of pecan pie ala mode.

An older man approached her and asked, "Are you the reporter from Denver, doing a story on Tony Sanders?"

Heather replied, "Yes. What can I do for you?"

The man said, "I'm Tim McAlester, you know, like the city." Tim grinned when he said this, thinking it was a cute statement. Heather did not know that there was city in Oklahoma named McAlester.

"Well, anyway," he continued, "I was Tony's best friend growing up. We played together as kids. We were best friends all the way through High School."

This peaked Heather's interest. She invited him to sit with her at her booth. "What was Tony like as a child."

"Oh, he was a ball of energy, and so was I," he said excitedly. "We rode bikes for hours. We climbed up most anything like trees, houses, buildings. We were kids. We were invincible. We had sleepovers at each other's house. Our parents hated it because we were wild and loud. We invented a game. It's called 'I think' and we roared laughing all the time."

"How did 'I Think' go? How did you play it?"

"Tony and I would take turns," he began, clearing his throat, "and say 'I think' and then make up some absurd event that we should both go out and try. I would say something like 'I think we should climb out the bedroom window, run out to the barn, climb up into the hayloft and jump down, then sneak back into bed.' We would both look at each other and say 'Naw, that's no fun.' And then we'd giggle for a while. Then he would create some adventure that was greater than mine, and we'd end with 'Naw, that's no fun.' Both of our parents were mad at us the whole time we slept over."

Heather enjoyed the childhood story. "Would you mind if I took some notes?"

"No. Go right ahead," Tim said. "Even through school we would hang around and play together and invent epic adventures. As we got older we included girls in our stories, and we always got the girl!"

Tim paused for a moment as the waitress brought Heather's food. He ordered coffee for himself. Then began again.

"In High School we were still best friends. But things were slowing down. I was mostly interested in girls. He was too, but he was interested in the girls that went to church with him. Some of those girls didn't go to our school. So we would spend our weekends apart, me with my friends and him with his church friends."

Tim took a sip of his coffee. "When we graduated from High School, we went our separate ways. Neither one of us was picked for the draft, you know, the war. So I went off to the University of

Arkansas and he went to a Christian College in Oklahoma City. We kept in touch. I was proud when he graduated from college, and he was proud when I graduated. He went off to a graduate school. I went into business with my dad. We were each other's Best Man at our weddings. He was a good man, and a good friend.

"You probably already know that Uncle Sam found out that he was an ordained minister. So they forcibly invited him to join the Army as a Chaplain. He had two kids and one on the way. But he obeyed his orders and went off to war."

Tim took another sip of coffee. He produced a face that showed Heather that he was sad and confused. She waited for him to speak again.

"When he came back from the war he was different," Tim explained. "On the outside he acted friendly and excited to be home. But I could tell that it was all an act. I suppose you heard his story of killing some enemy in Viet Nam. It took the joy out him. He got a church. He tried being a minister again. But it wasn't the same for him. I know he and his wife had problems because of what changed him.

But he stayed with her. He kept their marriage together. But he started living in the garage apartment."

Tim sipped coffee and went into deep thought. "You know; I would do anything for him. If I could figure out what to do, I would do it. I want to tell you something but I don't want you to think I'm bragging. I have made millions in business. And if there was something I could buy, some plan that I could pay for, I would do it in a heartbeat! The cost would be no barrier. I would gladly pay anything! He was my best friend growing up."

Heather thought for while on the things Tim talked about. "Tony said that the Christmas spirit, or whatever it is that he shows when he turns into Santa Claus, doesn't automatically stop on December 26th. He says it stays with him for up to a week after Christmas. Have you noticed this about Tony?"

"No, I never see him after Christmas," Tim said. "He pretty much goes into hiding until he emerges the next year as Santa Claus. And I got to tell you, he's a pretty good Santa Claus. Everyone loves him. I wish he could be happy the rest of the year, too."

Tim finished his coffee. He handed Heather his business card. "If you can think of something, anything, just let me know. I want to help." They exchanged pleasant good-byes and he headed out the door. Heather stayed in the café for a while to finish eating her dinner and to write more notes about her visit with Tim.

When she returned to her hotel room she typed some notes into her computer. She was mesmerized by that Mother Teresa Effect the doctor spoke about. She looked it up on line and was fascinated by the study. It was a Harvard medical researcher performing this experiment on his medical students. She also wrote down in big words in her notebook, "acts of kindness OBSERVED or PERFORMED." She filed it into her memory. She fell asleep quickly that night. She had become excited about eating the Thanksgiving meal with Tony's family.

THANKSGIVING WITH A WAR HERO

Heather arrived at Tony's house right around noon just like she was asked to do. There were several additional cars there, probably family members from out of town. Georgia saw her walking up the driveway, met her outside and gave her a gushy welcome.

"Hi Heather," she said loudly. "I am so glad you could come to our home for Thanksgiving. It'll probably be crowded. Looks like the whole family is coming."

Heather replied, "I thought you said just a few guests."

"Well, it's just our family, and you. So just a few...guests...and family." Georgia was bad at making up excuses. But she was happy.

Heather was assigned to the table setting duties. There were five tables set up in the kitchen, den, and family room. Some smaller tables for the younger grandkids. The sofas were lined with TV trays. She counted spaces for 65 people. "But just a few guests" she mumbled to herself, with a smile on her face.

Tony entered the kitchen about the same time that Heather went in to get more silverware. He was dressed in his usual drab clothes. He was sporting the same frown he wore when she first met him. He offered a grunted "Hello" to be cordial. He asked his wife, "When is dinner going to be ready?"

"You'll have to be patient, Honey. You know it takes us a while to get things ready." Georgia turned away from him after telling him to be patient. Then Tony started to grin. It was nice. She hadn't seen him smile yet today. He then sneaked over to the counter that had the desserts and took five cookies. He put his finger to his mouth as if to say "Don't tell

Georgia what I did." He then walked to the den and gave the cookies to four of his grandchildren and ate one himself. They all hugged him and ran out. He turned back around with that same smile on his face. He shrugged his shoulders. He couldn't help but sneak cookies for his grandchildren. Then he sneaked up behind Georgia and gave her a kiss on the neck.

"Oh, get out of here, you Casanova," she barked sweetly.

"Well, this is a side I've not seen in Tony," she said to herself. "I like it."

"Hey Heather," Tony said, "Come with me. I want to introduce you to my family."

"But I'm not finish…," she started to say.

Georgia interrupted and said, "Oh, go ahead. We'll finish up in here."

Tony led her through the maze of tables and chairs and led her out to the grand patio that adorned their back yard. "These are my sons, Steve and Tony Jr. They were already around before I…went out of town. And this is my only daughter, Rachel. She was born when I was, you know, out of town." He introduced Heather to several of the in-laws and grandchildren. "And this is my youngest son, Willie, or William. He was born, um, nine months after I came back from out of town."

Willie sported an embarrassed look. He said, "Dad looks forward to embarrassing me with that story.

"Well, you know that your mother and I still love each other," Tony said.

"Not in my world you don't," Willie responded.

Tony walked away with a smile. Then he introduced Heather to all of his grandchildren. He had to think about a couple of names, but he got them all correct. There were fifteen grandchildren. "I have two great grandsons around here somewhere. I'll introduce you when I see them."

One of the granddaughters grabbed Tony's hand and got him to play a board game with her and four others. He sat down with a big smile, asked about the rules, and what he had to do to win. Then he just joked with all of them over and over again. He was the life of the party. This was not the same man who screamed at her "I CAN'T UNSEE WHAT I

SAW THAT NIGHT!" He was happy, vibrant, alive with energy and joy.

Heather wandered back towards the kitchen to see if any other chores needed to be done. Everything was done. They just had to wait for all of the food to finish cooking.

"He sure is happy today," Heather said to Georgia. "He really enjoys his family."

"Oh yes," said Georgia, "Holidays, any holiday, brings him out of his shell. We all look forward to them. We all see the pre-war Tony."

"When the family goes home, does Tony stop smiling? Does he go back to being alone, not talking to anyone?" Heather apologized for being nosey. But she wondered about this wounded recluse who enjoyed wonderful family moments.

"No, the joy stays for a couple of days," Georgia explained. "I asked him one time why he lit up so much when family comes over. He told me that he can't believe that he was responsible for all these good people. Sometimes I catch him standing in a corner and looking at his whole family and just smiling. It's like he could stare for hours. He really loves his family." Georgia started to frown a bit. "Then he remembers the war, and that day. And he goes back to feeling that he doesn't deserve all the happiness. He goes back to Viet Nam. It replays in his mind. I used to watch him when he first starts to remember. I know when he gets to the part where he orders the killing. His eyes shut tight, he holds his stomach like he's getting sick, then he cries. It used to be a lot of crying. It seems the crying is easing. Then he has a violent outburst of tears. He won't leave. Part of him just can't come home from the war."

Georgia had to wipe some tears. She took a deep breath and said, "Well, at least for today he is putting it all behind him. He loves his family!"

The doorbell rang and several more people walked into the already crowded house. "More family?" Heather asked.

"No, these are neighbors and friends from town," Georgia said. "We always invite people we know who can't go out of town to see their own families for Thanksgiving. One year we had about a hundred guests for dinner."

Georgia took the time to introduce Heather to all of her guests. She met a doctor, a real estate mogul, even the Mayor and his wife. It seemed like Georgia got happier and more bubbly as each guest arrived.

When everything was ready, Tony called everyone to assemble on their grand patio. Georgia gave instructions on how they were to proceed through the serving line, where to get drinks, and where to sit. Then it was Tony's turn. He offered a short speech about how important family was. And he praised all the other guests as part of his family on that special day. Tony then offered an elegant, heartfelt, passionate prayer for family, friends, and food.

Heather was impressed at how Tony was handling himself. It was crowded and chaotic in his home, but he loved it. "This must be the real Tony, the one before the war," she thought to herself. "This is the Tony he needs to be all the time. I wish I could help."

When she said those words she felt a little sad. Many people have had that same wish for Tony to be whole again. But nothing has worked. She saw

Georgia walking towards her. She cleared her throat, brushed off imaginary crumbs from her dress, and forced a smile onto her face.

"Are you OK, dear?" Georgia asked quietly.

"Oh yes," said Heather. "I'm just watching Tony. He is different than when I first met him."

"This is the old Tony. My family loves the old Tony," Georgia said. "We all pray every day that the old Tony would return."

Conversations from all sides consumed the house. Heather eventually filled her plate and sat down next to the mayor and his wife.

"I understand you are the Mayor of Blackwater," she said after introducing herself.

"Yes I am," the mayor said excitedly. "I'm Bill Watson and this is my wife Mary. Now, you're the reporter from Denver, aren't you?"

"Yes, I'm here to do a story on Tony," she explained. "I know that many stories have been done on him but there are some facts that my boss said was missing from the other reports. So, I'm here to dig a little deeper."

"Well, good luck," Bill said. "If you can find something others missed, you will be our new local hero."

Bill went on to talk about how the city of Blackwater held a "welcome home" parade to honor Tony when he came home. "I remember listening to folks who were at the parade that day. He was cordial, alright. But everyone noticed that part of Tony was missing. They didn't see happiness on his face. That made people try harder to help him out of is depression. But nothing worked. Eventually people stopped trying. Now, we enjoy the Santa Claus that appears every year. And I think Tony enjoys it, too. But I sure wish I could find something or do something to help him out."

Heather leaned in and spoke softly, "He says that being the Santa Claus is part of his penance for what happened in the war. Do you know anything about that?"

"Yep, we've heard the story of what happened," replied the mayor in soft tones. "And I think that's why he pours his heart into the Christmas season. It makes him forget the past for a while. But the past, his past, never goes away."

The subject was changed as others sat down at the same table. The food was great and the company was wonderful. Heather had a great Thanksgiving dinner experience.

After dinner the two usual things happened: the television was turned on to football and the kitchen was stirred with cleanup. It was like living in the 1950s again. The men watched the football while the women cleaned the kitchen.

Heather stayed at Tony's house for a while after dinner. She enjoyed watching the kids and grandkids interact. She loved watching Tony as the loving dad and grandpa. "Of all the Thanksgiving Day dinners I have eaten," she said to herself, "I think this is my favorite." But how could it not be her favorite? Tony was the perfect host. He was the perfect patriarch. He was happy and made sure that everyone else was happy.

When others started leaving the party, Heather excused herself and went back to her hotel room. She opened her computer and started typing in some info about the dinner and the absolute joy that Tony displayed.

As she was typing away, her cell phone rang. It was her boss, Randy Smith. "Oh, what does he want now?" she muttered to herself before she answered the phone.

"Hi Randy," she said. "Happy Thanksgiving!"

"Hi Heather," he replied. "The same to you. I hope you had a good day."

The two exchanged some pleasantries. Randy was feeling a little guilty about sending her off to cover a story over a holiday. But Heather knew that he called to see how the story was going.

"So tell me about this perfect Santa," Randy said. "Is he for real? Is it an act? Can people see through his façade or is he just that good of an actor?"

"Oh it's real," Heather responded. "Everyone I've interviewed swears he is the real thing. Kids love him. He remembers everyone's name from year to year. He puts his heart and soul into the experience."

"I wonder why he is such a perfect Santa?" Randy questioned. "Why does he put so much into it? Other people who play Santa do a really good job, too, bringing joy and happiness and all that stuff around Christmas. Any idea on why he goes overboard, why he does more than any other Santa?"

"Well, I'm no psychologist," said Heather as she began to explain what she thought, "but I think his going-overboard on Christmas is related to how awful his experience during the war hurt him."

Heather went on to explain Tony's story, the short version. He was a trained minister. He had an idealistic view of people and the general goodness of people everywhere. He enjoyed the ministry because he could help people. "Tony put his entire heart and soul into the ministry. And from what others said, he was very good at it."

She told Randy about the draft, graduating from Chaplain's school, and being shipped off to Viet Nam when his wife was pregnant with their third child. Even then his heart was set on helping soldiers through the horrible experiences of war. "They gave him the rank of Second Lieutenant. But he wasn't trained as a soldier. He did have to walk with, work with, eat and sleep with the soldiers. That was not his life, but he did what he could."

Heather then told Randy "the story" that changed Tony forever. She told him how his patrol was ambushed. Many of them died. Tony was unconscious and wounded. When he woke up he saw his buddies who were dead. The others were gone. He walked aimlessly through the jungle until he ran across four US soldiers who were also walking aimlessly. They had also been attacked and five of their buddies were captured by the enemy. Seeing that he was an officer, they asked Tony to help. They found their buddies that had been captured. Tony devised a plan and gave the order that killed five enemy soldiers. "Tony also fired a rifle that night. He killed one of the enemy soldiers. And, it was Christmas time. December 10, 1969."

She went on to report that he and nine soldiers walked through the night. When they got back to base they were cheered as heroes. A photo taken that night was seen throughout America. He received the Purple Heart and was flown home. The President gave him the Medal of Honor. All of the fanfare soon faded. Tony wasn't interested. All he could think about was how he ordered the execution of five enemy soldiers.

Heather also told Randy about what the psychologist said. Tony had seen the extremes of two opposite worlds: ministry in which people love and help each other and war in which people hate and kill each other. When these worlds collided on that cold December day, Tony's mind could not process what happened in a healthy way. "That's why he views the Christmas season as a time of penance. He had experienced the most horrible event in war back then, so he wants to make Christmas the most perfect experience today."

When she finished telling the story the phone was silent. Randy was in awe of what he heard. After a few moments Randy was able to form a question.

"So, he's been in a depression for almost fifty years?" he asked. "And he magically comes out during Christmas and plays Santa?"

"Pretty much," Heather replied. "As long as his mind fails to process the war in a healthy way he will continue to view Christmas as a time of penance. The rest of the year he lives in his depression."

Randy was silent. Then, "Is there any hope? Have you seen any bright moments in his life?"

"Yes," said Heather. "I was told that the Santa Claus was very real, genuine. And his family said that the joyous feelings and positive actions don't stop immediately after Christmas. It lasts for two or three days, sometimes up to a week after Christmas."

Heather told him about Thanksgiving dinner at Tony's house. "I saw a wonderful man today. He was genuine. He was the perfect host and the perfect father and grandfather. I asked his wife if he went back into his depression right after Thanksgiving. She said that the good stuff stays with him for a couple of days after his family leaves."

"Hmm, both of those stories have the same ending," Randy surmised. "Tony acting, or genuinely becoming a giver of joy changes him for not just the day or the season, but it stays with him for a while. I wonder if that's the key to helping him out of his depression. Maybe he needs more of these kinds of things in his life."

Heather said, "So, if he had more of these kinds of experiences it might push him over the edge? Push him back into the old Tony, the pre-war Tony? That makes sense. But how? I don't think we can have Thanksgiving more than once a year. And Christmas only happens once a year. And I don't know if his whole family can get together more often. But your hunch seems to be valid. I'll keep swirling that in my mind and see if I can come up with anything."

The phone conversation ended and Heather typed a few more notes into her computer. As she laid down to sleep she kept thinking about how she could arrange some activities that would help Tony be more of his old self to push him over the edge. But that seemed daunting. Then she thought, "Maybe there can be one or two events of such great magnitude that it would reverse what that one horrible event in the war caused?' One great event? Is it possible? What could we do?"

Heather had started down a new path of thinking. She was still no psychologist. But sometimes fresh thinking or looking at something with a new set of eyes has caused great things to happen.

THE LIGHT BULB COMES ON

When Heather awakened on the morning after Thanksgiving she was surprised at how much noise there was outside her hotel room window. She opened the curtains a crack to see what was going on. Lots of cars were going past the hotel. Lots of people were walking up and down the main street of Blackwater. "I guess this is Black Friday in Blackwater, Oklahoma," she spoke softly to herself.

After she dressed she went down to the café to get some breakfast. Tina, the waitress, greeted her with her usual bubbly attitude. "Howdy, stranger! Missed you yesterday for the Thanksgiving dinner."

"I told the waitress on Wednesday night that I was invited by Tony's wife to have dinner with them," Heather responded. "I couldn't say no."

"That's OK," Tina said. "Mary told me that you came in to cancel your reservation. I'm sure you had a much better meal with the Sanders than you would have had with us."

Tina poured some coffee then ran off to seat other customers. Heather took a sip. It was good coffee. Her mind was already churning, trying to come up with ideas on how to help Tony. Now that Thanksgiving was over, she had twelve days before December 10th when Tony would crawl into a hole and relive that awful day during the war. That was her self-imposed deadline. She was going to find something she could do before he could disappear from his family and fight the war alone.

While she was waiting on her food to arrive, she opened up her computer and began a search for information on how anniversary dates effect PTSD patients. Maybe there would be some ideas she could use. She found the usual sights written by psychologists and about things that would trigger a patient to go back to a horrible time. She found that triggers included sights, smells, a phrase someone would say, the face of some stranger that reminds of people in one's past, and anniversary dates.

"Hmm, here's something interesting," she thought to herself. "It says here that anniversary dates can remind the patient that it was the day their life transitioned into a different life, a different outlook on life, a transition from hope to hopelessness, or even horror. Well, that's Tony. That was the day he transitioned from life saver to life taker. Hmm. It also says that many PTSD patients intellectually know when a traumatic episode is coming and feel guilty when they give in to it. But their body's memory takes over and they return to the trauma they are trying to escape."

She thought for a moment. And she apologized to herself and to any mental health professional that might be reading her mind at the time. But then she thought, "So before 1969, December 10th was just a usual day in Tony's life. Then on December 10, 1969 something traumatic happened that changed his view of December 10th. Hmm," she hummed to herself, "if one event radically changed him, maybe another single event can change him again. Too simplistic? Too elementary? Too pie-in-the-sky dreaming from a reporter?" Even then her logic seemed good to her, at the time.

She left the café and went for a walk through the downtown area of Blackwater. She enjoyed the specialty shops and thrift stores. She enjoyed watching people buy things and describe how happy a loved one might be when they open the present. It was Christmas-time in small town America.

She walked past the local library. It was the Sarah Witcomb Memorial Library. They were having a book sale inside. So she went in. There were a few people inside, but not many. The reporter in her was curious about the woman after which the library was named. When no others were around she walked to the librarian and said, "Hi. I'm from out of town. Can you tell me about Sarah Witcomb, the name on the library sign?"

"Oh, of course," replied the librarian with a smile. "I'm Esther Riley. You're the reporter from Denver coming to do a story on Tony Sanders. He's a wonderful man. I just wish he could get out of the depression he's in."

She shuffled a couple of books on the table then answered Heather's question about Sarah Witcomb. "Sarah was an old lady who lived by herself most of the time I knew her. She had a modest home. It's over by where Tony lives. We never saw much of her family. But they did come about three or four times a year and take her to Oklahoma City where most of her relatives lived. She was born and raised here in Blackwater and so were her children. She was an only child so she didn't have any siblings. When her husband died the children wanted her to move to The City but she just wanted to stay where she was comfortable.

"She was a humble woman. She always cared about others. She would make things for others like dinners and clothing. Always had a smile on her face. She was good inspiration for the rest of us.

"About ten years ago she died in her sleep. The neighbor who always checked in on her found her and called the family. They had the funeral here in Blackwater at the Presbyterian church. It's a very large building and I was worried that there wouldn't be very many people at the funeral. But it was packed. Many of the town's people were there. And it turns out that there were about a hundred relatives there, too. She had four children, I think about twenty grandchildren, and too many great grandchildren to count. And of course there were the marriage partners of the children and grandchildren. It was a huge family.

"It turns out that Sarah had a small fortune from her husband. She willed part of it to the town. That's how we got this new library. The rest of course was for her family. But that family! We were all surprised at how big it was. Just imagine if she had two or three sisters and they all had huge families, too. This town couldn't have held such a big crowd."

Esther chuckled a bit as she thought about how big of a family there might have been if Sarah had siblings. She went on and told Heather some other stories of her own remembrances of Sarah. Heather took notes on all of the stories. It would make a great story of its own.

After the library Heather continued to walk and shop in the main street area of the town. When she eventually arrived at her hotel room she opened up her computer and typed in the notes she had taken that morning. She was amazed at how big Sarah Witcomb's family had gotten. Heather began figuring out how big her own family had become. Even though she didn't live near any of her relatives, she loved them very much. She counted around fifty relatives in her immediate family, from her parents down to their one and only great-granddaughter.

Then her thoughts went to Tony and his family. "He can't understand the blessing of saving nine soldiers during the war. And his own family, he loves them and they make him so happy that the good feeling sticks around for a few days afterwards. And the people he makes happy when he is Santa Clause, there must be hundreds. And that good feeling sticks around for a while."

She stopped typing, took off her reading glasses, and thought about Tony's situation. "He likes people. People make him happy. His happiness hangs on for a while even when the people leave. It's the anniversary date. That's the problem." She thought about it some more. "I wonder if the solution to Tony's depression is to rework December 10th, replace the old memory with a new one? It would have to be some big event to be able to replace such a horrible memory."

Heather seemed encouraged by her train of thought. But she also cautioned herself not to get too excited. If professionals haven't thought about this, maybe it's not such a good avenue to go down.

She decided to pay another visit to Georgia Sanders. She wanted to explore Tony's large family and how it affected him. It was an avenue she needed to go down but didn't know what she might find. She gave Georgia a quick call and drove towards her home.

When she arrived Georgia was out on the porch waiting for her. She ran over and gave Heather a big hug and ushered her into the house.

"I am so glad you called," bubbled Georgia. "Most of our family left last night and it seems rather quiet around here." She got up to get the whistling kettle off of the stove, poured some hot water into a cup with a tea bag in it, and gleefully brought it to Heather. "So, tell me what's on your mind today."

"Thanks," said Heather as she acknowledged the hot tea. "I wanted to ask more questions about how Tony looks at his large family. I remember you said something like he doesn't feel he deserves such a good family. Is that close to what you said?" Heather put her tea cup back on the saucer and reached for her note pad that was packed in her purse.

"I think I said that Tony doesn't think he deserves to be happy," said Georgia sheepishly as she offered this slight correction. "He loves me and the whole family. On special occasions he really comes out of his shell. You saw it yesterday at our family dinner. And even today he is doing well. But that war has too tight a grip on him. No matter how wonderful his family is, and how much fun he has with the family, in his mind he keeps going back to Viet Nam and that horrible day. The horror he saw has a stronger pull on him than the love of his family."

Heather pondered her next question. She took a sip of her hot tea, cleared her throat a little, and then asked, "Do you ever talk him about your family when the happiness stops? Wow, that was a bad question. Of course you have talked to him over the years about this.

When you talk to him about family when he reverts back to his depression, what does he say, what does he do?"

"I really don't talk to him much anymore when he goes into hiding," she explained. "I used to do it all the time. I love him so much that I felt I had to try to get him to see how wonderful his life really is. And how he is responsible for every happy member of our family. But he didn't want to listen."

"You said that you don't talk to him much anymore about all this," Heather said. "Why have you stopped?"

"In the beginning he would get out of control, yelling and screaming at me," Georgia said with a tremble in her voice. "He would say things like 'You don't understand' or "You weren't there'. He would always come back later and apologize for his behavior. And I think he is aware of how badly he talks to me. But something else takes over and he just goes off. After a few years we both decided that it would not be good for me to keep urging him to replace remembrances of the war with remembrances of family. And he doesn't want to keep hurting me. So we agreed that I would bring it up just every-once-in-a-while." She paused to take a sip of her tea. "That's when he decided to live in the apartment above the garage. He knows what's going on in his mind. He doesn't like it. But he can't control it. So for the sake of our marriage, for the sake of our family, he started living apart from us."

Georgia started tearing up. Heather pushed the tissue box closer to her. She reached out and touched Georgia's hand. She needs to have someone listen to her. She didn't go to the war but she is re-fighting it every day, just like Tony does. Heather let her have some time to regain her composure.

"I have another question for you," she said softly, so that she wouldn't catch Georgia off guard. "Tony has replaced the war with family on Thanksgiving. Looks to me like he had a really good time. And, from what I hear, Tony has replaced the war during the Christmas season, at least from December 11th through the 25th. I can't wait to witness for myself the world's most perfect Santa. It's just that one dark day, December 10th, that Tony has not been able to replace. If it is as simple as a 'replacement', do you have any ideas on what we can do to help him? And if we were to come up with something, would he be willing to even come out of hiding to participate?"

"For the most part we leave him alone on December 10th," she said. "Dr. Billings told us to give him that time to himself. As long as he is not a danger to himself or someone else, he needs that time to process the ugly event. But I have had to get his help on December 10th now and again. He is always willing to come out of his apartment if I ask him and if there's something important to do."

Heather went deep into thought. Georgia noticed that she had zoned out for a few seconds. "What are your thinking?"

Heather replied, "I know that when I want to come up with an idea on how to change something, I start making a list. Maybe that's what we need to do."

She adjusted her notepad so that a clean page appeared. She wrote "What Happened" at the top of the page.

"That's easy," said Georgia. "He killed an enemy soldier."

Heather wrote that down. She thought for a moment. Then she wrote on her notepad "What Changed?"

She sat up in her chair and said, "We need to figure out everything that changed at that moment in Tony's life. Most of these will be negatives but we need to list them out."

Heather and Georgia went back and forth. They came up with a list of changes that affected Tony's life. Here's what they came up with:

- Tony helped rescue five soldiers BUT he didn't feel good about it

- In all ten soldiers walked out of the jungle BUT Tony felt no joy and no hope

- Tony came home to a happy and loving family BUT the happiness did not last

- Tony witnessed the growth of his family through children and grandchildren BUT he felt he didn't deserve such happiness

- Good Change: Tony enjoys his family on Thanksgiving and the good feelings last for a short time

- Good Change: Tony enjoys interacting with family, friends, and strangers from December 11th through December 25th

It was a short list, but it covered all the things that Heather had personally witnessed.

"Oh, here's one more for the list," Heather interjected as she broke the uncomfortable silence. "Tony has successfully replaced the war with two special events, Thanksgiving and Christmas. But he goes back to the war as soon as those holidays are over." As she paused she clicked the end of her pen between her teeth.

"What about the men Tony rescued?" Heather asked. "Has Tony ever had a reunion with them?"

"Not that I can remember," said Georgia. "He just hangs around the house, hiding from the war, hiding from reality."

Heather and Georgia continued to talk for another hour or so. They tried to come up with some ideas that might help. Heather wrote them all down. But none of the ideas had the "wow" factor. None of them jumped out to them.

After the nice time she had with Georgia, Heather headed back to her hotel room and started typing notes into her computer. She typed in the list that the two women created. Still no great idea jumped out at her. She typed in the notes she made about Sarah Witcomb, the woman who gave money for the library. Heather giggled to herself while typing in these notes. "Wow. Everyone thought she was alone in the world. Then, POW, one hundred relatives appeared out of nowhere. That must've shocked everyone." She typed in the statement that Georgia made about Tony. "He thinks he doesn't deserve to be happy." With that note she stopped typing.

Heather's mind went back to the photo of the ten men that walked out of the jungle that night. It should have been a time of relief, a time of celebration. But Tony had already been thrust into hopelessness. It was that moment, feelings of hopelessness, that colored the rest of his life.

"But there were ten of them" Heather said out loud. She remembered what Tony said after his doctor reminded him that he saved five soldiers, and a total of ten soldiers walked out of the jungle that night. "Tony immediately had dismissed the ten. Tony had already made up his mind that nothing good was ever going to happen because of that night."

Heather's voice was getting a bit louder with each sentence. Excitement was brewing. An idea was forming. "He keeps seeing the one enemy soldier that he killed. And he has yet to see, really see the lives of the ten that walked out of the jungle."

The idea exploded into her mind. She excitedly grabbed her notepad and launched out of her hotel room. She had become a soldier on a mission. And when Heather Smith, Channel 21 News-Denver, gets an idea, there is no stopping her.

THE PLAN IS HATCHED

Heather headed straight to Tony's house. She wanted Georgia to be the first one to hear what she had in mind. While she was driving she wrestled through her purse to find the business card that Tim McAlester gave to her. She remembered it had his personal cell phone number on it. She dialed his number frantically as she was driving. "He has to be in on this plan. He said he would pay anything to help Tony."

Tim's cell phone went directly to his voice mail. Heather figured he wouldn't answer a call from a strange area code. She left a message after the beep.

"Tim, this is Heather Smith from Denver," she explained excitedly. "I have an idea about how we can help Tony. You must call me back as soon as you get this message. We have only twelve days to put all this together. I'm headed over to Tony's house to talk with Georgia. Please call me immediately. Thanks." Though her phone number was undoubtedly on his caller ID feature, she gave him her cell phone number anyway.

It didn't take long for her to get to Tony's house. Blackwater was a small town. One could easily get anywhere within five minutes or so, unless there is a slow train moving through town. No trains stopped her. She arrived at Tony's house expecting to see Georgia sitting on her porch. But she wasn't. But as soon as Heather exited her car Georgia was coming out of her house to greet her.

"Well, welcome back to our home," Georgia said with an excitement of her own. "What brings you here today?"

"I think I have an idea about how to help Tony," Heather said as she walked hurriedly up the sidewalk. "I wanted to run it past you to see what you think. Is Tony around?"

"He's in his apartment like usual. I don't expect to see him until midafternoon. That's his usual schedule."

"Good," Heather answered in a somewhat hushed tone. "I don't want him to hear about this. If my idea sounds good, it's going to require a lot of people working hard in the next few days. The whole town needs to get behind the plan. But we all have to keep it a secret."

Georgia was intrigued. The women went into the house. Georgia already had hot water ready on her stove for hot tea. She brought tea and some cookies to the table. Then Heather unfolded the idea for her.

"The gist of the idea is to replace the horrible memory of what happened during the war on December 10th with a new and beautiful memory on the same date this year." Heather was talking quickly as she could. She could hardly contain her excitement. "Tony has already replaced the horrors of war with a beautiful family gathering at Thanksgiving. He's his old self on that day. He chose to be happy and leave the war behind, at least for one day. Then he replaces the war by becoming the perfect Santa from December 11th through the 25th. Even though he explains it as his 'penance' for what he did, he still chooses to be happy and leave the war behind. And after both of those events the happiness lingers for a few days or so. So what if we were to replace December 10th with something so beautiful that it might 'shock' Tony into loving life and being happy for the rest of the year?" Heather stopped to take a sip of hot tea. "Here's my idea. What if we were to...."

Someone called Heather on her cell phone. She looked at the number and displayed a huge smile. It was Tim McAlester returning her call. "Tim, I'm glad you called. I have an idea. Can you come over to Tony's house right away? Thanks!" She didn't give time for Tim to say much. But he was on his way to the house.

"Tim McAlester is coming over," she told Georgia. "He said he would be willing to do anything and pay anything to help Tony." Heather gave an excited squeal.

"Great," said Georgia. "What is this great plan you have?"

"Family is the answer! You two have a wonderful, large family. It is wonderfully chaotic when you all get together. At least that's what I saw. But it was beautiful. So here's what I was thinking." Heather paused for a few seconds for a sort of dramatic effect. "When Tony arrived back at his base on December 10th, he had already decided that nothing good was ever going to happen to him again. He had already dismissed the idea of being a hero to nine soldiers on that day. And when he came back from the war he tried, he really tried to be a good husband and father to you and the kids." Georgia shook her head in agreement. "And then your family just kept growing. And even though he says he doesn't deserve a big, beautiful family he lets the family make him happy on special days." Heather pause for another dramatic-effect moment. "Families happen!"

Georgia sat with a courteous smile on her face but her eyes announced that she was confused. "Where are you going with all this?"

Heather explained. "Over the years you two grew from a small family to a large clan. Life happened! Family happened! On December 10th in 1969 Tony dismissed any benefit that he provided for those nine rescued soldiers. The horror closed his mind and his heart to that. But what if we were to show Tony that life happened for those nine, too? What if we were to show him that over the last fifty years or so that family happened for them, too? You two have a large family now. If we were to find those soldiers, Tony might be able to see hundreds, maybe even a thousand happy, healthy family members. We can show him that it wasn't just nine soldiers that he saved that day. He saved generations of people because of his heroic act. That's the memory he should have. It may be so powerful that it will replace the horrible memory of what happened that day."

Georgia's eyes lit up. "Tony loves his family. He thinks he doesn't deserve to be happy. But those other men. They deserve to be happy. And Tony is responsible for their happiness. Wow. It just might work!"

Georgia stood to give Heather a big hug. The two women hugged and cried together.

Just then the doorbell rang. It was Tim McAlester. After bringing him some hot tea the two women excitedly told Tim of their idea. "We have just twelve days to pull this off. We'll have to offer travel money, hotel and food vouchers for all of the guests. Some will drive here and some may have to fly here. You said you would pay anything. It's going to cost a lot of money. What do you think?"

Tim grew a huge smile on his face. "Let's do it!"

Ideas started flowing from all three of them at the table.

Heather: "We need a place to host this big celebration. Will the weather be good enough to do it outside at the park?"

Georgia: "The weather will be perfect. I can call the city and reserve the park. What will we call our event?"

Heather: "Hero Homecoming. What about lodging for all of the guests?"

Tim: "I can call the local hotels and see how many rooms will be available. What about the city people? Will everyone be invited to this?"

Heather: "Absolutely. Tim, can you call the mayor and see if he can help get the word out. Remember, it's a secret. Let them know."

Tim: "Got it!"

Georgia: "Should we provide a picnic feast for the crowds? How many should we expect? Who should we call to provide the food?"

Heather: "Call all the restaurants in town. See if they can cater for a couple of hundred people each. Maybe they have food trucks. We can give food vouchers to the families of Tony's army buddies. Everyone else can pay for their meals."

Tim: "We're going to need busses or provide rental cars for the guests arriving at the airport in Tulsa. And we're going to need an accountant to help keep all the receipts straight from all the guests. I'll have my guy do all this."

Heather: "We need to find those nine soldiers that Tony helped rescue. Where can I go to get that information?"

Tim: "The VA will have all that info. And I have Dr. Billings' personal phone number. I'll call him and tell him you need his help on this today!"

The exchange of ideas took about an hour. All three of them were taking meticulous notes. They all had tasks that they volunteered for or were asked to do. By three o'clock the trio left Tony's house to go work on the "Hero Homecoming" celebration that was to take place on December 10th.

When Heather sat down in her car she opened up her cell phone to take another look at the newspaper picture of Tony and the other nine soldiers returning to camp that day. She read the part of the story that was showing. No names besides Tony's were given. The bottom of the article indicated that it was continued on a separate page. Her first task was to go to the library and see if she could get the whole article.

When she arrived at the library she found it open but empty of patrons. It was Black Friday and school was out. The library was not a popular place when there was shopping that had to be done. She saw Esther Riley, the librarian, right away. "Hi,

Esther. I need to know if you have a copy of the newspaper article about Tony and the soldiers coming back to camp. I took a picture but part of the article was continued on another page."

"Yes, I think I do," replied Esther. "Most of our old newspapers are on microfiche so I know I have a copy there. But we saved a few of those from the war. Tony was our local hero. Let me run to the back and find it for you."

Esther disappeared into the back of the library. But she wasn't gone long. She reappeared with a yellowed copy of the newspaper dated December 12, 1969. Tony's picture was on the front page. Heather was very careful as she opened up the almost 50-year old newspaper. She turned to page nine where the article continued. And there the names were. She took a picture of the continued article. Opening up her notebook she quickly scribbled the names of the soldiers that were present in the picture.

Of course there was Second Lieutenant Chaplain Anthony R. Sanders. The other soldiers were listed in order of rank. It also gave their hometowns.

Sergeant Steven F. Warner, Houston TX
Corporal Ryan N. Stubblefield, Atlanta GA

Private Jonathan P. Steele, Oklahoma City OK
Private Robert M. Adams, Milwaukee WI
Private Stephen S. Stewart, Englewood CO
Private Samuel D. Eider, Fayetteville AR
Private Michael D. Andrews, Phoenix AZ
Private Jim R. Smith, Langston OK
Private Malcom F. Rogers, Tallahassee FL

The soldiers were from all over the US. She figured that would be the case. Then, her cell phone rang. "Hello, this is Heather."

"This is Dr. Billings. Tim McAlester called and said you needed help finding the soldiers that served with Tony. Tim said it was urgent. He told me a little about your plan for Tony. I'm driving my wife home right now. It won't take too long. But after that I can meet you at my office in about half an hour. Is that good for you?"

"Absolutely!" Heather replied. "I'll see you in half an hour."

When she was satisfied with her list, she turned to thank Esther Riley for all her help. She gave her a hug and told her to keep December 10th free on her calendar. She left the library and drove directly to Dr. Billings office. She arrived fifteen minutes before her appointment. But she had nowhere else she wanted to go. She was too excited to not be there at the moment he arrived.

As soon as Dr. Billings arrived, Heather bolted from her car and met him on the walk up to his office building. "Thank you so much for helping us out on this project."

"I'm glad to do it," he replied. "Tim told me about the project and I am intrigued. Your logic is right on track." He opened the door to his office building, disarmed the alarm panel, and led Heather down to his office.

When they were inside his office, Dr. Billings said, "I have a couple of concerns about what you are planning to do for Tony. First, I want to make sure that you are not just doing this for a story. I guess I'm hoping that you really care about the health and well-being of Tony. He would be terribly hurt if he found out that he was just a story."

"Fair question," said Heather. "I was sent to find the real story behind the perfect Santa. That's true. But what I found was more than a story. Tony is a wonderful man with a wonderful family. This whole town is concerned for him, too. This is way more than a story. And I am personally invested in what it will take to help Tony get back to his old self."

"Very good answer. I'm glad to hear that you care about Tony," he said. "The second concern is for you. Many people have tried for years to help Tony, to get him back to the old Tony. And we have made some slow progress over the years. My concern is this: if this does not work, or if this does not bring the results you have in mind, I don't want you to be devastated."

Heather thought for a moment. She had not thought about what would happen if this plan did not succeed. "Well," she began, "I guess I hadn't thought about it not succeeding. But my instinct is that it will help. I appreciate the caution, but I must push this plan through."

"Sounds good," he said. "I wish you all the luck. If it's OK with you I would like to be there just in case Tony has a negative response to what happens."

Dr. Billings pulled up a second chair to his desk so that Heather could watch as he searched for the soldiers in her picture who were with Tony.

Heather handed him the handwritten note she made at the library. He started with Sergeant Steven F. Warner. The VA records found him immediately. "Says here he was drafted into the army in 1964. He was awarded the Purple Heart during his first tour of Viet Nam. He recuperated and was promoted to Sergeant. He did a second tour of duty starting in 1968. After the war he continued to the 20-year mark. He retired as a Master Sergeant. He was originally from Houston TX and he now lives in Plano TX. Here's his address and phone number."

Heather quickly wrote down all the notes she heard about Sergeant Warner. She decided he would be the first soldier she would contact. "If I can get him on board," she thought, "the others will come on, too."

Dr. Billings turned to the second name on his list. "Let's see, Corporal Ryan N. Stubblefield. He was awarded the Purple heart. He continued to serve in Viet Nam. Then…." He stopped for a moment. "They list him as KIA, Killed In Action. He never made it home from Viet Nam."

Heather felt a pain in the pit of her stomach. She had become attached to Tony and his family and had felt empathy for him, his family, and anyone who took part in that war. Hearing the news about Corporal Stubblefield made her feel as if she herself had lost a loved one.

Dr. Billings continued down the list. Of the seven privates listed in the newspaper article, six of them were found in the data base as living in various parts of the US. The one exception was Private Jim R. Smith from Langston OK. He also was KIA. He did not make it home from the war. She grimaced when she heard news about him.

Heather had a list of the seven living soldiers who were with Tony that night. She remembers that Tony called three of them Curly, Shorty, and Stewart. She didn't know which one of the real names of the soldiers belonged to Curly and Shorty. But she figured that Stewart was actually Private Stephen S. Stewart.

"Thank you so much, Dr. Billings," she said when their computer search was over. "I will start contacting these men tonight. I appreciate all your help."

"Your welcome, Miss Smith," he replied. "But let me give you another caution. The men you are going to contact saw the same things that Tony saw. Don't be surprised if one or more of them do not want to participate in this Hero Homecoming. Don't be discouraged if they choose not to remember that day."

With this caution fresh on her mind she left the doctor's office and drove back to her hotel. In her room she opened up her computer and began typing notes. She was thrilled to have the information on the soldiers. She grieved for the two who did not make it home. When she was done typing her notes, she grabbed her cell phone so she could start calling the soldiers. But then her mind went blank. "What am I going to say to them?" she thought. "How do I explain to them who I am and why I have their information?" Then realizing that her cell phone number might come across to them as sales call or a robo-call, how could she make those men feel at ease in taking to a complete stranger about something that happened almost 50 years ago?

She took a few minutes to rehearse what she would say. At one time she started typing notes into her computer. When she was satisfied with what she would say she picked up her phone and put it to her chest. "OK. This is going to work. Let's do this…for Tony!"

She dialed the phone. After two rings the call was answered. It was a man's voice on the other end. He said, "Hello…?"

SUMMONING THE SOLDIERS

Heather's hands were sweating. She doesn't get nervous very often. But this is not just a news story in which she has to check facts. This is a real human story. She's emotionally involved. She cares for Tony and his family. She indeed wants to help him get to the point of accepting what happened, in a healthy way, and move on with his life. This first phone call is one of seven she needs to make before the night is over. She dialed the number, it begins to ring. After two rings someone answers. It's a man's voice. "Hello...?"

"H-Hello," she responded nervously. "I'm, um, Heather Smith. I'm a reporter from Denver. Is this Steven Warner?" The man on the phone hesitated, then said that he was Steven. "I'm calling about Chaplain Anthony R. Sanders. Do you remember him from your time in the army during the Viet Nam war?"

Steven cleared his throat. Still hesitating he offered some "ums" and "ers" trying to figure out why some reporter from Denver wants to talk with him. "I remember Tony. Is there something wrong? Is he sick? Did he die?" His voice changed from hesitation to concern.

"Tony is OK. He is alive and living in Blackwater, Oklahoma," Heather explained. "I'm calling because Tony is still in a big battle with PTSD that he brought home from the war. I was sent to do a story on him. There have been many stories written about him. But no one seems to be able to get to the heart of the matter and help Tony adjust to life after the war. That's what I'm trying to do. I've come up with a plan. I'm hoping it will work, but I need your help."

Steven began to speak. "Tony saved my life one night. I'm sure your heard the story. I had been in the army for about five years. I was a sergeant. I had been in many combat situations. But as I remember than night, I was plenty scared. The Viet Cong ambushed us. It was a wild gun fight. I lost two men that night. Five of my patrol were captured. I started walking around with four of my soldiers trying to find help. It wasn't supposed to be that way. I couldn't just leave my men there. We came across the Chaplain in the middle of the jungle. He was lost. Said his company was ambushed. Several casualties. Many dead. The rest of the company chased the Viet Cong. He was alone. He was afraid. We all were. I was glad to see an officer, even if he was just a Chaplain. He came up with a plan. We found our men, killed five Viet Cong, and went back to camp. I heard he got the Medal of Honor. I continued in the army for several years. So, what happened to Tony after the war?"

"Tony was sent home to rehab in the VA hospital in Washington DC," Heather said as she helped Steven understand Tony's story. "He rejoined his family, even went back into ministry. He had a local church in Blackwater OK. But he was haunted by what happened that night. He was not a soldier.

He was a minister. He keeps seeing the face of the soldier he killed that night."

"He surprised me" he continued. "He may have been a minister, but he was sure a good shot. Hit the guy right in the head. He saved my men. He saved us all that night. I thought he would be proud."

Heather said, "That's the problem. He was a minister, trained to save souls. That night he became a sniper, and he took the life of another human being. For almost fifty years now he has wrestled with that scene in his mind. It doesn't help him to remember that he helped save nine lives that night. All he knows is that he killed someone."

Silence on the other end of the phone. Finally, "So, what's your plan? How does it involve me?"

Heather scanned her notebook for the notes she took when she and Georgia and Tim were frantically planning a celebration for Tony. "I have spent some time here in Blackwater. And I have seen a couple of times when Tony allows good events to make him happy. He becomes like his old self, before the war, before that night. Something is getting to him. My thought was that if we could create a fantastic event that showed Tony how much benefit he gave to you and your men and the world, that event might help replace the horror of the night in the jungle."

"Makes sense," said Stephen. "What do you have in mind?"

"Well, first, tell me about your family. Did you get married? Did you have children and grand-children? How many people did you give life to when you came home from the war?" Heather was trying to come up with a huge number of people who are alive and doing well because Tony rescued those soldiers.

"I was single when Uncle Sam drafted me," Steven said. "After the war I went home and continued in the Army for a while. I wanted to get my twenty years in. Took advantage of the GI Bill and got an education. Found a woman who tolerated me. Got married and had four kids. She left me after about six years of marriage. Said I was not gentle enough to her or to the kids. She was probably right."

"You had four children," Heather continued. "Did they all get married? Did they have children?"

"Yep, they all had children. I have quite a fertile bunch of kids," Steven explained. "Every one of them had four or five kids each. So I figure I have eighteen grandchildren from my kids. There's another five grandchildren from second marriages. Both of my sons divorced and then remarried. My older son married a woman with three kids and my younger son married a woman with two kids. That makes four kids and twenty-three grandkids."

Heather chimed in. "You also have son-in-laws and daughter-in-laws and former daughter-in laws. That's about six more in your family. Are any of your grandchildren married?"

"I think maybe five or six of them are married. No great grandkids yet," he said.

"I've done the quick math. With four kids, twenty-three grandkids, six or so children-in-law, five spouses for your grandchildren, plus you and your ex-wife, that's forty all together. Does that sound right?"

"Sounds pretty good," he said. "But I did get remarried a few years ago. My new wife had an already built-in family. So you could add another twenty or thirty people to my family."

"OK. That's what I'll put down for you," she said with wonderment. "Here's the plan we have in mind. We want to get as many people related to the ten soldiers that walked out of the jungle that night as possible. We want to show Tony that even though he took the life of one man, he is actually responsible for the lives and happiness of hundreds more people. We have a man here in Blackwater who is willing to pay all the expenses for you and your entire family to come here for a celebration for Tony. He will pay for your gasoline, plane tickets if anyone needs to fly here, your food, hotel rooms, and anything else associated with getting your whole family here. But you have to be here on December 9th. That's only eleven days from today. The celebration will be on December 10th. That's the anniversary of that horrible night in the war."

Heather and Steven talked for a while longer. The more they talked the more excited Steven became. He finally said, "He saved my life that night. I would be glad to help him get his life back."

Heather wrote down that Sergeant Warner would be there and would bring as many family members as possible. They exchanged emails. Heather committed to keeping in touch with him to see how many family members would be able to come with him. She said she would arrange all of the funds that he needed for his family. Sergeant Warner lived in the Plano TX. Most of his family lived in the Dallas area. He said that most will probably drive to Blackwater.

Her next call was to Private Jonathan P. Steele. With her first phone call out of the way Heather had confidence as she spoke with Private Steele and the others on her list. All of the soldiers on the list gladly accepted the invitation to be in Blackwater for the celebration for Tony. She knew that not all of the family members would be able to attend. But she added the total number of possible attendees. She estimated that it was close to four hundred and fifty people. And even if only a fraction of those actually showed up, along with the towns people the crowd would be huge.

She reported back to Georgia and Tim concerning her phone conversations. Details started adding up on their "to do" lists. Tim started the process with his accountant for arranging prepaid gas cards for those who would be driving. He got his travel agent to start looking for the best airfare prices available for those who had to fly in. Georgia began to work on spreading the word around town about the celebration. She was also in charge of talking to the café where Tony went every day for dinner. They had to be part of the celebration but they couldn't say anything to Tony. Keeping an entire town quiet so that Tony would not be aware of what they were doing would be the biggest task for all three. Heather made notes on calling the Mayor, reserving the park, and contacting restaurants to have food trucks at the park on December 10th.

Then next day Heather woke up early. There were now only ten days to go. She was too excited to sleep in. She had several emails from the soldiers who served with Tony. They told of how many family members they already contacted. The news was good. Most family members committed to being in Blackwater to honor the man who saved the lives of the family patriarchs. She estimated in her mind that already almost one hundred and fifty people would be there.

While Heather was eating breakfast in the café, Georgia showed up to eat with her. She was bubbling over with excitement. "Oh Heather, I hope you don't mind," Georgia began apologetically, "but I made phone calls to the local VFW and to the High School. The VFW said that they would assemble a color guard of veterans to "Present the Colors" at the celebration."

"That is fantastic," replied Heather. "I'm glad you thought of that."

"I also called the High School yesterday and talked with the band teacher," Georgia continued. "I asked him if he could have the band march and play at the park. He said yes!"

Again Heather excitedly thanked Georgia for thinking of that detail. But Georgia wasn't finished. She had more to say.

"Today I'm going to sit down with the High School principle," she said. "I used to babysit him and his brothers. I'm going to tell little Scotty that he needs to dismiss school that afternoon so that they can all be at the park."

Little Scotty was actually Scott Hanson, a good-looking man who stood over six feet tall. But to Georgia he would always be Little Scotty.

Tim showed up at the café that morning as well. He reported that he started working on vouchers for gas and airfare. He gave his office assistant the duty to call all the hotels in town to hold as many rooms as possible for the out of town guests. He also arranged for shuttle busses to pick up guests at the Tulsa Airport and bring them to town.

Things were going great on this the second day of planning for an event that would hopefully change Tony's outlook on life. There were many more things that had to be done. But this trio of planners were satisfied that the plan was working and that December 10th would from that time on be seen as the day when Tony started leaving the war behind.

While they were eating, Heather noticed a man picking up a copy of the local newspaper at the front counter of the café. She was a bit worried about keeping the news away from Tony.

"Does Tony watch the news on TV?" she asked Georgia.

"No. The TV in his apartment has a DVD player attached," she said. "He just watches videos of old TV shows from the 1960s. Mostly westerns and sitcoms. He doesn't get live TV up there."

"What about the newspaper?" Heather asked as she motioned to the man who had just picked up a copy of the paper. "Does he read the local newspaper?"

"Yes he does," Georgia replied with a small gasp. "He always picks it up here and reads while he eats. He does the crossword puzzle and other word puzzles in it."

"Is your paper a daily newspaper?"

Georgia said, "No, it comes out once a week, on Fridays."

Heather looked at the calendar on her phone. "That means there will be one more issue next Friday. I for sure don't want to ask the newspaper not to print anything about the December 10th celebration, but we need to make sure that Tony doesn't see a copy of it next week."

"I'll make sure Tony doesn't see the paper next week," Georgia said. "I can talk to the manager and have him hide the papers when Tony comes in. And there is a convenience store that Tony walks past on his way home. I'll get the manager to hide the papers there, too. I'm sure they will cooperate."

"Well, is there any other possible ways that Tony can get news from now till December 10th?" Heather asked.

Tim and Georgia both indicated that Tony would not seek out other outlets for news. He was quite a recluse and didn't really want to know what was going on around him. "Even when he reads the paper, he mostly skips over the news and goes to comics and puzzles in the back," Georgia admitted. "But we'll make sure he doesn't see the paper at all next week."

With assurances flowing freely from each of the trio of planners, they all left to continue working on the celebration. For the next few days they met regularly to discuss details, share info on who might be coming and who won't be able to come. All in all, things were going smoothly.

It was Friday, December 6th, and only four more days to go before the celebration. Tony left his apartment at about four o'clock to walk to the café for his evening meal. Everything he did was predictable. You could set your watch by Tony's actions. It never varied. Heather was at the café watching for Tony to arrive. She wanted to make sure that the manager hid the newspapers. There was an article about the celebration on the front page. In Heather's estimation it was a well-written article. But it didn't need to get into Tony's hands.

When Heather saw Tony walk up to the café, she took her usual booth that was on the opposite side from where Tony usually sat. That way she could keep her eyes on him. She wanted to leave right before he did to make sure that the newspapers were out of sight if he chose to go into the convenience store for a copy.

Tony complained about the café not having any newspapers. But he got over it quickly and just ate his dinner. Heather finished her dinner, paid her check, and went out to her car. She drove past the convenience store and warned them that Tony would be walking past their store at any time. They hid the newspapers behind the counter.

Just like Georgia predicted, Tony walked into the convenience store and asked for a newspaper. He was disappointed. With a scowl on his face he left.

Heather was watching him from her car. About two blocks away from the store Tony stopped and looked down the street towards the park. He was looking at something. "Oh no, I forgot about the park," she thought to herself. "I hope they're not setting up the celebration yet." Tony stood on the corner for a few moments. Then he turned and walked towards the park. Heather drove her car to the corner where Tony turned. She rolled down her window and heard machinery running. She watched as Tony arrived at the park. He looked around for a couple of minutes. Then he turned to walk back to his house.

Heather called Georgia and told her that he took a detour to look at the park. Georgia said that she would talk to him and see if he was suspicious of anything.

Heather drove her car and parked it about a block away from Tony's house. She could see Georgia coming out of the house to greet Tony.

"Hi Honey. How was your dinner?" she asked.

"It was fine, but they didn't have any newspapers left," Tony scowled. "That's the first time that happened to me. And then the store didn't have any copies either. Is the newspaper falling apart?"

"I hope not," responded Georgia.

"And then I noticed some goings-on at the park," he said. "They're doing some mowing and some painting. It's December, for crying out loud!"

"Well, Honey, I think the High School has some event there this weekend. They're probably just getting the park ready for them." Georgia hated to fib like she did. But the High School would be there this weekend. They will be practicing their routine for Tony's celebration.

Tony went into the house and off to his apartment. Georgia saw Heather in her car down the block. She flashed a thumbs-up sign to her and went into the house.

Heather breathed a sigh of relief. A small crisis had been averted. "Only four days to go," she thought. "I hope nothing else happens that would give away this secret planning for the great celebration."

PLANS COME TOGETHER

With three days left until the Hero Homecoming celebration the entire town of Blackwater was in a stir. Everyone knew that all the details and everything that was happening was to be kept from Tony. Heather, Georgia, and Tim all reminded the people to be especially quiet around 4:00pm each afternoon. That's when Tony left his home to walk to the café. He would be back safely at his home by 5:30pm.

It was Saturday, December 7th. There was a small parade in the downtown area of Blackwater. It was to honor WWII veterans on Pearl Harbor Day. It was an annual event. Tony made it a point not to leave his home on that day. He didn't want to see people celebrating such a disaster as the bombing of Pearl Harbor. He didn't mind that others did it. But he would not be part of it. That day Georgia usually fixed one of his favorite meals for dinner so he wouldn't have to go out. So Saturday came and went without causing Tony to wonder what might be going on. The next two days would be a different matter. Sunday and Monday would see the arrival of a few hundred out-of-town guest for Tony's celebration. Keeping all that quiet would be difficult.

Heather had arranged for a camera crew from her news station in Denver to cover the celebration. They arrived Sunday afternoon. Heather made sure that they were put up at a hotel on the other side of Blackwater. She didn't want Tony to accidentally see it driving through town on one of his walking trips. The news van was impressive. It had two satellite dishes on the top. The sides were painted to include Channel 21 News in Denver in bright colors so no one would confuse their van with other news stations. It was parked at a hotel on the other side of Blackwater. But it was only five minutes away.

Heather was at the café a little before 4:00pm on Sunday, December 8th. She watched for Tony to arrive for his usual evening meal. He arrived, just like clockwork, and sat down at his usual booth. Heather sat and ordered some dinner on the opposite side of the café.

About 4:30pm a large group of out-of-towners arrived at the café. They were a bit noisy. But they had just ended a three-hour road trip to get to Blackwater, or so she gathered as she was eavesdropping on the group. "Oh, I hope they are not here for the celebration already," she muttered to herself. She strained to listen to their conversation. "Hey Tina," Heather called out in a whisper to get her attention. "Can you sit that group over on this side of the café? I think they're here for the celebration and Tony's here, too."

Tina, the bubbly waitress, nodded in agreement and went over to take care of the new customers. They were seated at three tables that were put together to accommodate a big party. Tina asked the leader of the group to come with her to meet Heather.

"I want you to meet Heather," Tina said in a low tone so as not to attract Tony's attention. "She's a news reporter from Denver and she is in charge of Tuesday's celebration."

"Glad to meet you," said Heather as she extended her hand to shake his. "Would you sit down for a second, please. I need to let you know that the man we are going to honor on Tuesday is in the café right now. I don't want your group to say anything about what we will be doing on Tuesday."

"Oh sure, I understand. I'm Joe Bonner. My family and I just drove in from Ft. Smith."

"Pleased to meet you," Heather said kindly. She remembered that one of the men that was with Tony that night was originally from Arkansas. She guessed this family was related to that man. "So, are you related to Samuel Eider?"

"Yep, he's my grandfather," Joe replied. "He'll be coming tomorrow sometime. I grew up in Tulsa. We came early to see some Christmas lights. They have some big displays around here. We'll probably go by Rhema Bible College in Tulsa.

Maybe tomorrow we'll go out to Yukon to see their lights. They really know how to do Christmas."

Heather got assurances from Joe that he and his family would not talk about the celebration as long as Tony was in the café. But he would be leaving at 5:15pm sharp. His activities were very predictable.

When Tony left the café Heather decided she needed to talk with Georgia about Tony's dinner on Monday night. There would be many more guests in town tomorrow and many more chances of Tony hearing about the celebration. She waited about half an hour before leaving the café. She wanted to give Tony enough time to walk home and then go to his apartment.

When Heather arrived at Tony's house she saw Georgia sitting on the front porch. The two women met in the driveway, as usual. They went into the house and Georgia brewed some hot tea for her guest. After some pleasantries, Heather talked about her concern for Monday night.

"We had a family arrive about 4:30 today from Arkansas," Heather explained. "They came to eat at the café and Tony was there. I was worried that they were here early for the celebration. I had the waitress sit them on the far side of the café so Tony could not hear what they were saying." Heather pause to take a sip of her hot tea.

"I'm worried about tomorrow," Heather continued. "There will be many more families arriving. The stores will be full. The restaurants will be full. I don't want Tony finding out about what we're doing. Is there any way you can keep Tony at home tomorrow for dinner?"

"Well of course," Georgia replied. "I can fix him his favorite dinner, hamburgers and French Fries. The only reason he goes out for dinner every night is because I don't like to fix basic food you can get anywhere. But Tony doesn't like variety and he doesn't like change. But he loves my hamburgers. I'll take care of that."

"O, bless you," Heather smiled. "Now, just for my own sake, how are you going to get Tony out of the house Tuesday to go to the park?"

"He is not opposed to coming out of his apartment on December 10th," Georgia explained.

"There was this one year that one of the grandkids was having a Christmas concert at her school. And, I know you're not supposed to have favorites, but little Gloria is his favorite. He went to the program. Now, he complained a lot, but he went. I just need to give him a story that will make him want to go to the park. Don't worry."

When Heather left Tony's house she was confident that Georgia would be able to get him to the park on Tuesday. At least that part was taken care of. But there were many other details that had to be worked on.

Tim McAlester had set up a welcome table at the same hotel where Heather's camera crew was staying. All of the families who were coming to help honor Tony were instructed to check in at the Hampton Inn. There they received food vouchers for meals. Their hotel rooms were paid directly by Tim. Each of the guests, relatives of those men who were rescued by Tony during the war, were told that the vouchers were like money. "Just go to whatever restaurant you like and let them know you have a voucher for your meal. Give the card to the waitress and we will pay the restaurant later." Each family also received a map of Blackwater OK. They also received a drawing of the park and the general area where their family was to gather on Tuesday. They wanted to keep the families together.

When Heather arrived at the Hampton Inn she saw that everything was going smoothly. She had her camera crew meet her in the coffee shop at the hotel to discuss the logistics of the celebration. She also told them to spend Monday filming different parts of Blackwater, including the stores, museums, and the crowds that were gathering. They were to go to the park as well to get a feel for the area. Heather gave them a drawing of the park and showed them where Tony would be when he would arrive.

The plans for the celebration were finalized in Heather's mind. Tony would not enjoy any kind of formal presentation or ceremony of any kind. He was opposed to being honored in public. The plan was to have him meet the men he served with at one corner of the park. Then each of the men would take him and introduce him to their families.

There would be a ceremony of sorts on Tuesday. At 11:00am sharp the color guard from the VFW would march into the middle of the park and present the colors. The High School marching band would already be in place. The presence of the marching band would signal to the crowd that the flags are coming. When the color guard made its presentation, the High School Band would play the Star Spangled Banner. It would be simple, patriotic, and a wonderful honor for a war hero that never got over the war.

Heather was hoping that the crowds would help Tony realize that his actions on that horrible day in 1969 actually gave life to hundreds of people. In her mind everything would go well. And Tony would somehow let go of the horrible past and embrace the present. She was confident it will work. When Heather Smith sets her mind to do something, it will get done.

The next day, Monday December 9th, Heather went to the park to see how things were going. When she arrived crews were already setting up tables and chairs. Each family would be assigned to a certain picnic shelter, each having four picnic tables. More tables and chairs were set up around the shelters to accommodate all of the family members.

At the open end of the park many more tables and chairs were set up. But there was still a lot of room for families from Blackwater to set up folding chairs and watch as their kids enjoyed the open space or the large playground on the south side of the park.

Two large banners were set in place. Neither one of them had Tony's name on it. He never liked the fanfare. One banner read, "We Live Among Heroes" with the US Army logo on the bottom. The second read, "US Army. Guardians of Freedom." Both of the banners were supplied by the Army Recruiting Center in Blackwater.

On the east side of the park workers were using paint to mark off the places in the grass where the food trucks would be set up. There would be ten or so trucks to choose from. Electricians were running wires to each site. There were also spaces for other kinds of vendors. Heather and the organization committee wanted to make this a community fair atmosphere. They wanted people to enjoy the day and stay for a while. On the west side of the park workers were unloading PortaPotties. The brand name for the portable bathrooms was Honey Bucket. Heather just shook her head. It was cute and gross at the same time.

About that time the High School Marching Band entered the park. Heather made sure that her camera crew was filming this dress rehearsal for the band and the color guard. The band's instructions were to assemble at the Blackwater Baptist Church that sat across the street from the park. They were to march in at the proper time playing a couple of peppy songs they usually played at football games. Heather wanted the home town crowd to hear some familiar songs.

She was amazed at the band. They were in full uniform. They were regal and elegant. Everyone who was working at the park stopped to watch. When they arrived at the center of the park the band divided itself into two groups. Each group formed a semicircle. There were gaps on both sides of the circle for the color guard to enter and exit. The two semicircles faced each other and stood at attention. About four city workers with spray paint cans marked the edge of the circle. This would help the band return to the exact position the next day and to help keep visitors from occupying the space until the band left. The majorette gave the signal and the drums started sounding. It was a cadence the band director came up with.

At the edge of the park, the same place from which the band entered, stood the color guard in full uniform. By this time all of the workers stood and watched as the flags were being presented. Heather told the camera men to get footage of the workers watching the band come in. The human interest side of the story was what Heather wanted to capture.

The color guard consisted of six soldiers. The two on the ends carried rifles. The four in the middle each carried a flag: the US Flag, a POW/MIA Flag to honor Viet Nam Veterans, the State of Oklahoma Flag, and a Flag of the City of Blackwater. They marched in single file to the middle of the circle formed by the band. The drums ceased as the color guard reached the center. One soldier barked orders for the soldiers to stop and turn. Three flags were lowered so that the US Flag stood tall by itself. Then the band played the Star Spangled Banner. Most of the people at the park sang along with the band. When the song was complete, the crowd cheered like they do at ball games. Heather was amazed at how powerful the simple presentation had come off. She was tearing up as she witnessed the event. "This is going to be great!" she said to herself.

As Heather turned to leave, a large satellite truck from the Fox News Station in Tulsa drove up. They had heard that Blackwater was going to have a big celebration for a local war hero. Their editor sent the truck to see if there was a story for their market. Heather walked over to visit with the news crew.

"Hi. I'm Heather Smith from Channel 21 News in Denver, an ABC affiliate," she said graciously. "Are you here to do a story on Tony Sanders?"

The junior newsman shook Heather's hand and gave a big smile. "Hi, Heather. I'm John Garcia from Fox News in Tulsa." He pointed to the large logo and colorful painting on the side of the truck. "Yes, we heard about the celebration that's happening tomorrow. We wanted to get a feel for the area and the people to see if this would be something we wanted to cover."

Heather was glad to talk to John about the plans for the celebration. She did not necessarily want her story to be an exclusive. She didn't mind sharing information. She just wanted the celebration to be so fantastic that Tony might be able to have a new and beautiful memory for December 10th every year.

"I'm kind of new to news reporting. I usually get sent out on out-of-town stories and fluff pieces," John said.

Heather told him that she, too, was still in that category even though she had been with the same station for about five years. "It will get better," she assured him. John was appreciative of the information Heather shared with him.

Heather continued to check on plans that were being made throughout town. She went to the café to see if they were having an increase of customers. She could hardly get in the door at the noon rush. There were so many extra people in town. She saw

Tina from a distance and waved to her. Tina gave her a thumbs up sign. Other restaurants were experiencing the same things. It was good for Blackwater. And it was good for the plans. More family members will hopefully mean a greater impact on Tony when he sees the crowds.

Heather stopped at the Hampton Inn to see how many of the soldiers' family members had checked in. It was a zoo in the lobby of the hotel. It was crowded and chaotic. But everyone seemed to be in a good mood.

Tim called Heather over to the registration table. "We already have three hundred and thirty family members who have checked in. If we continue at this rate, we'll have over five hundred guests related to the soldiers who served with Tony." Tim was grinning from ear to ear. This is what he wanted for Tony. This is what he wanted to fund.

Heather spent the next few hours checking in with businesses to see how things were going. All of the business were quite busy with customers. But they didn't mind. This was a good "shot in the arm" for Blackwater's economy.

As the sun was going down she decided to grab a meal from the local Arby's Restaurant and take it to her hotel room. While she was eating, she took out her computer to browse the list of things that needed to be done. The guests were arriving in droves. The park was getting set up. The restaurants were filling up. Tim already called all of the food trucks and other vendors that were to be at the park. They were all coming. The band was ready. The color guard was ready. There was not going to be formal presentation of any kind. So, no microphones or speakers were needed. It seemed that all the plans were being met. She smiled as she closed her computer.

She turned on the TV in her room. She clicked through the channels until she came to the Fox News Station from Tulsa. Sure enough, there was John Garcia giving a short teaser about the celebration in Blackwater that would happen the next day. Heather gave a quick evaluation in her mind on John's story. "He looks comfortable. He speaks well. And he's getting his audience excited about the possibilities for tomorrow. Good job, John!"

Heather could not think of one other detail that she had to check on. She watched a couple of shows before she went to bed. She set the alarm on her phone and crashed on her pillow. Exhausted she fell asleep quickly. But she smiled hoping that…no, knowing that tomorrow would be a good day for Tony. It might just be the thing that brings him home from the war for good.

THE HERO HOMECOMING

Heather woke up at 6:00am. It was Tuesday, December 10th. She sat up on her bed with a smile. She was amazed at how in just two weeks she went from not knowing Tony Sanders at all to a day when an entire town would come together to celebrate the great war hero. She was also amazed at how she talked with Tony's patrol who were with him in the jungle that night forty-nine years earlier. She was amazed at how many out-of-towners would be at the celebration in the park today.

She headed to the café for a good breakfast. Sitting in her booth she went over the itinerary for the day's events. "Let's see," she spoke to herself, "the police will be closing down streets around the park at 9:00am. My camera crew will be at the park at 9:00am sharp. They haven't let me down yet." Heather was punctual and expected everyone else to be punctual as well. "The families of the service men will start arriving at the park around 9:00am, too. They were all told that Tony would arrive at 10:00am. The seven servicemen will be at the northwest corner of the park at 9:30am. So if their family members are slow to get there, that will be OK. Georgia will talk to Tony around 9:30am and tell him something that will get him out of the house. Tony and Georgia should arrive at the northwest corner of the park at 10:00am. Easy!" She chuckled to herself. At least on paper everything would fall together easily.

But getting Tony to the park might not go smoothly. Georgia was a very persuasive woman. But Tony was a deeply depressed veteran. Besides getting him there, she knew that any number of things could go wrong or the right things could happen but not according to the "schedule" that she arranged. Now she began to fret and worry. But she was used to that kind of inner atmosphere in her brain. That's how she approached most of her responsibilities.

When she finished her breakfast she drove over to Tony's house. She wanted to visit with Georgia to see what story she had come up with to get him out of his apartment on the darkest day of the year.

It was a little before 8:00am when Heather pulled up in front of Tony's house. And, as usual, Georgia met her halfway up the walk and greeted her with the usual bubbly welcome. "Come on inside," Georgia graciously demanded. "I have some coffee on."

"I'll have to skip the coffee," Heather replied. "I just finished breakfast at the café and have had plenty."

When the women sat down at the table Heather asked, "So, what kind of story did you come up with to get Tony out of the apartment and to the park?"

"Oh, you don't have to worry about anything," Georgia said confidently. "I'm just going to tell him that our kids are at the park and that something happened. When he asks for more information, I'm just going to ask him to trust me. Even though we don't live under the same roof, we are still husband and wife and would do anything for each other. I'll have him at the park at 10:00 sharp, or close to it."

Heather could have done without the "or close to it" part. But she left the house confident in Georgia's ability to persuade her husband to do almost anything.

She headed straight to the park. It was almost void of people. Just a few city workers taking care of smaller details. There were policemen walking around getting ready for the crowds. And about 8:45am, people started to trickle in. Most of the early comers were locals with folding chairs staking out spots in the park for their own family and friends. About 9:00am some family members of the service men began to arrive. Heather had assigned some people from the Chamber of Commerce to be there to guide people to their family areas. There were four shelters that had been built in the park. Heather had ordered four large tent-like shelters to be set up as well. Each of the servicemen had a shelter reserved for them and their families. Tony's family was assigned to an area as well. Tables and chairs were also set up around the shelters to accommodate the whole family.

At 9:00am Heather's camera crew arrived in their brightly colored satellite van. She knew they would be there but she gave a sigh of relief when they showed up. The Fox TV truck from Tulsa also arrived about that time. Heather showed each crew where to park and set up.

By 9:30am the park was beginning to fill up. Food trucks were showing up and getting ready to welcome hungry guests. The locals were coming in from all directions. The family members were arriving and finding their areas. Heather enjoyed seeing the family reunions that were taking place.

The service men who served with Tony started arriving. Heather went down her checklist. By 9:45 all seven of them had arrived and were waiting at the northwest corner of the park with Heather. Each was dressed in civilian clothes. Each sported a ball cap that read "Viet Nam Veteran" on them. They were having a reunion of their own. Most had not seen each other since the war. She gave them time to shake hands and hug each other. They remembered funny things that happened in the midst of the horrible war.

When her watch chimed at 10:00am Heather interrupted the soldier's reunion to offer some last minute instructions. "I am so glad all of you could be here this morning," she began. "I am hoping that your presence here will give Tony a jolt, so to speak. And I want you to spend time in this area getting reacquainted with Tony. But then I want each of you to introduce him to your families. He's stuck on helping just nine men on December 10, 1969. I want him to see that nine men multiplied into hundreds with your wives, children, and grandchildren. I am hoping that he can see that what happened that night resulted in the beautiful happy lives of hundreds of your own family members."

After Heather gave the small pep talk the veterans huddled up to talk about how they would welcome Tony to the park. It looked to her that they were coming up with something special. But then she looked at her watch again. It was 10:10am.

Tony had not yet arrived. Her instant-worry faucet started dripping in her brain. But right then she received a text on her phone from Georgia. "On our way. Be there in five minutes." She told the veterans that Tony would be here in just a few minutes.

Heather made arrangements with the local police to escort Tony's car to the northeast corner of the park. She heard sirens in the distance. A police turned the corner towards the park. Tony's car followed the police car. Another police car trailed behind.

Heather turned around to let the veterans know that Tony was arriving. She saw the veterans standing in a line with their feet apart and hands behind their backs. She later found out that this was their At Ease stance.

When Tony exited his car he just stood motionless. He saw Heather. Then he looked at a park that was overflowing with hundreds of people that he didn't know. Georgia walked around to his side of the car and talked to him. She urged him to walk with her. Tony limped with a cane in his right hand. Slowly he walked across the grass that led to where Heather stood. He looked at her and then looked at the old men who were standing in a line just past her.

Heather took a few steps towards Tony. "I found some old friends of yours," she said. "They came to talk with you today."

Tony had a confused look on his face. He was staring at the first man in the line. Heather thought that Tony might have recognized him. She held her hand out towards the group of men, encouraging Tony to go talk to them.

As Tony approached the line of men, the first man in line hollered, "Attention!" All seven men stood tall, feet together, hands at their sides, looking forward. The first man in line turned slightly towards Tony and gave a salute. "Retired Sergeant Steven Warner at your service, Sir!"

Tony looked dazed. It took him a few seconds to drink in what was happening. Then he stood tall, transferred his cane to his left hand, returned the salute, and said, "As you were, Sergeant!" as he tried to remember military protocol from his days at the Chaplains School.

"The men are ready for your inspection, Sir!" said Sergeant Warner as he stepped back into line.

Tony walked to the man standing next to the sergeant. "Good morning, Sir!" he said as he gave a salute. Tony returned the salute.

"What's your name, son?" Tony asked.

"Private Robert Adams, Sir! You might remember me as Curly." The man took off his hat to show his red hair.

Tony went to the next man down the line and asked, "What's your name, son?"

With a salute he said, "Private Michael Andrews, Sir!"

Tony squinted at him. "Shorty?" he asked.

"Yes Sir!" he replied. Tony was quite confused because the man standing in front of him was not short at all. "Had a late growth spurt, Sir!"

Tony went down the line and talked with each man present. When he was done, he said, "Sergeant, there were nine men that day. I see only seven. Where are the other two?"

"Corporal Stubblefield and Private Smith are not with us today," the sergeant explained. "They did not make it home from Nam."

Tony scanned the faces of the seven men who stood before him. A tear had made it down his face. "I sure am glad to see you today." Tony started crying. The men broke ranks and huddled around him. There were lots of hugs.

When Tony "came up for air" he looked at the crowd of people that had filled the park. "Sergeant, who are all those people?" The sergeant pointed to a shelter in the middle of the park and said that those people were his family. Each of the veterans took their turn at pointing out their families. Tony was able to point to his family also. Private Michael Andrews took Tony to the area where his family was sitting. It was the closest shelter to where they stood. After that, Tony made the rounds to meet all of the family members of all of the veterans.

Heather saw that beautiful smile on Tony's face that she had seen a couple of times before. She told her camera crew to tape as much as they could of Tony meeting the family members of those he served with during the war. He especially liked meeting the small children. It was a wonderful thing that Tony experienced. Heather was hoping in the deepest part of her heart that this overwhelming flood of loving people would be the thing that would bring Tony closer to acceptance of what happened during the war.

The marching band from the High School had assembled on the east side of the park. And at 11:00am sharp they began playing and marching to the center of the park. The school fight songs were familiar to the local towns people who gave great cheers for what they heard. After two songs, the band went silent. The drum corps of the band began a slow cadence. The color guard had arrived at the east side of the park. They marched in single file, walking in step with the cadence of the drums. Everyone in the park stopped to watch. Everyone was silent. When the color guard found the center of the park, the center of the circle made by the marching band, they marched in place. The drum cadence stopped. Silence.

The leader of the color guard barked orders. "Company halt! Left face! Present arms!" At that point the soldiers with the rifles stood at attention. The US flag stood tall. The other three flags were lowered. The band played the Star Spangled Banner. Everyone in the crowd joined in to sing the words of the National Anthem. A roar of applause filled the air when the song ended.

For the next couple of hours Tony met the family members of the veterans. There were lots of hugs and kisses. He never stopped smiling the entire time. When he was finished with meeting the veteran's families, he walked through the park to do the same with the locals. He knew most of them because of his yearly Santa Claus activities. But he loved getting to know them better.

After a while Tony had to sit down on a park bench that was off by itself away from the crowd. He was tired and overwhelmed. But he was very happy. Dr. Billings approached Tony and asked if he could sit with him for a minute. Tony gladly accepted his presence.

"All this is for you, Tony," the doctor said. "And Heather Smith is the one who spearheaded this reunion for you. She wanted you to see how many people have been blessed by you, by what you did that day during the war. Ten people walked out of the jungle that night, including you. And those who made it home started families. Your family multiplied, too. Because of what you did that night, hundreds of people are alive, healthy, and happy. This is your legacy. This is what you need to focus on. This is what you need to remember."

Tony was tearing up as the doctor spoke. "Yah, I know," Tony said. "That was a horrible night." The doctor was amazed that for the first time he could talk about and remember that night without coming unglued. "I never realized how many people have been effected. I figured I didn't deserve my big wonderful family. But these guys did deserve their families. This has been a good day."

Tony and Dr. Billings had a good conversation. It wasn't like the sessions at his office. It was more like two friends just talking and sharing, reminiscing about the past and its troubles. But Tony seemed to have begun a new outlook on life. The doctor was cautiously optimistic. But to Tony it felt like the start of something big.

As the two were talking on the bench, Tony saw a young boy walking with his parents towards him. The parents stopped about twenty feet from the bench. Then with a little urging the little boy walked up to him.

"Well, hello, young man," Tony cheerfully said. He guessed that the boy was about four-years old. But he just stood there and didn't say anything. He was very nervous.

The boy's mother walked up to him and put her hands on his shoulder. "My son told us that he wanted to talk to you." Then turning to the little boy, she said, "Go on. Tell him what you told us."

The little boy looked at Tony and said, "Um, thank you for saving my grandpa during the war."

Tony kindly responded, "I was glad to do it."

Then without prompting, the boy took two steps backward, stood at attention, and gave Tony a salute. He was so surprised by the boy's action that he sat for a moment not knowing what to do. Then

Tony stood up, put his cane into his left hand, stood at attention, and returned the salute. When Tony and the boy put their arms down, the boy ran up and hugged Tony's legs. He ran back to his parents. The mother silently mouthed the words "Thank you" to him and walked away.

Tony sat down and cried. Dr. Billings put his hand on Tony's shoulder and smiled.

The interaction between the boy and Tony was captured on tape by Heather's camera crew. When she watched it later she broke down and cried, too.

The celebration had come off without a problem. Everyone seemed to be enjoying everyone's company. The food trucks did a brisk business. Some brought picnic lunches for their small families. But all in all everyone had fun and everyone was well fed. Tony spent the rest of the afternoon talking and hugging everyone he could. The smile on his face never faded.

Heather walked by the area where Tony's own family had gathered. Tony gave her a big hug. "I understand you are the one responsible for this chaos today," he said with a grin. "I thought I told you not to try and help me."

"Well, I didn't start out trying to help you," she said. "But the more I talked with people and the more I learned about you, this was the natural next step. I didn't even know if it would work. I didn't know if this would turn your life around or if it would increase your depression. But this happened because I started caring about you. Don't be mad."

"I'm not mad. I want to adopt you," he said that brought both of them to laughter. "Tomorrow I'll start my Santa Clause thing. But this year it seems to be a little different."

"Different?" she asked. "How?"

Tony smiled and said, "I'm not thinking about penance, at least for now. I'm thinking it's just going to be a lot of fun."

Heather said, "Won't it be fun to find out?"

The two embraced. They made plans to have breakfast together at the café in the morning.

When the day was done Heather went back to her hotel room, exhausted, and began typing notes into her computer. She smiled as she thought about the possibility of Tony's life being changed by the new and improved version of December 10th. She fell asleep quickly. She was looking forward to seeing the Perfect Santa Claus in action.

CHRISTMAS COMES HOME TO STAY

When Heather woke up she was already excited about the perfect Santa arriving in Blackwater, Oklahoma. She cautioned herself because she knew that what she would witness out of Tony today would be the usual Tony in his usual perfect Santa role. The real proof of whether the Hero Homecoming worked to help him out of his depression would not be seen until after the holidays were over. But she was excited about seeing Blackwater transform from a sleeping small town to the area's major Christmas destination.

Heather's plans were to stay in town one more day. She wanted her camera crew to get shots of Tony doing his thing. She would also be putting together her report for Channel 21 News-Denver.

She had arranged for her camera crew to eat breakfast with her at the café. They were to follow Tony and film him helping carry groceries, helping to put up Christmas decorations, and Santa talking to children. She also told them to get some interviews with the locals on tape. There was still a lot to do for her story to come together. It would air on her station that night.

As they left to go find Tony or Santa, Heather paid her tab at the cashier's station. Tina was the cashier. "Have you seen Tony today?" she asked.

"Oh yes," Tina replied with a giggle. "He's already been here. I think he started out at 6:00am this morning. And he's in full Santa uniform with a big smile and a jolly disposition."

Tony wasn't hard to find. He was in the downtown area of Blackwater meeting people with a smile and handing out candy canes to the children. He was hugging everyone he saw and posing for selfies with whomever wanted a picture. He was a bundle of energy. Everyone he met left with a smile.

The town was already setting up the Christmas Village in the park near the gazebo. Santa's chair was the center of the attraction. The note on the sign said that Santa would be there at 5:00pm to welcome the children. "That would be the perfect last shot for my story," Heather thought. "I'll have plenty of time to edit the film and go live tonight."

The FOX News station truck was parked near downtown Blackwater. Heather watched as they also filmed Tony and interviewed happy children and parents. She also noticed a camera crew from Oklahoma City and two or three more crews from other towns near Blackwater. "Tony is famous!" she exclaimed to herself. "People DO come from miles around to see the perfect Santa.

At one point she saw Tony walking with a group of small children towards a toy store downtown. Heather got his attention and asked if they could meet for lunch. "I'll see you at noon at the café," he said in haste as he was being dragged by the enthusiastic crowd of four and five-year olds.

Heather stopped two of the mothers that were following the crowd of children to interview them. They raved about how wonderful a Santa Tony was. They claimed that he was the best Santa they had ever met. One of the women said, "I know that Santa isn't real, but if he was, Tony would be closer to the real Santa than anyone in the world."

When Tony left the toy store a woman came up to him and asked if he would hold her three-month old baby so she could get a picture. Tony agreed and took the infant into his arms. The baby cried as she realized that a stranger was holding her. But Tony, the grandfather in him, was able to calm her down and put a smile on the baby's face. Heather thought, "Well there's another 'perfect' thing I can put on his list. He's the perfect Santa, the perfect hero, and the perfect grandpa."

Heather and Tony met for lunch. He sat at her booth wearing his full uniform. And to Heather, his outfit was the best she had ever seen. It was immaculate and worthy of the perfect Santa that wore it. They were constantly being interrupted by people wanting to say "Merry Christmas" or "Thank you" or for requests for pictures. Tony was genuinely impressed with people. His "Merry Christmas" or "Your welcome" were returned with enthusiasm. And he never turned down a photo opportunity. Heather was worn out just watching him and his endless source of energy.

When they had a moment without crowds surrounding the table, Heather asked, "How are things going today?" When Tony quickly answered that everything was fine, she qualified her question by asking, "I mean, are things any different today than they were in years past?" Heather knew that on this, the first day of the perfect Santa, that Tony might not be able to distinguish much difference. But she was curious if his outlook this year was different.

"It's too early to tell," Tony said. "Like I said last night, I'm not really thinking about penance too much. But the proof will be after Christmas. I'm thinking I'll have a different post-Christmas attitude, but I'll just have to wait and see."

Heather nodded in agreement right before a large family approached the table. It was Sergeant Warner's family. They wanted pictures with Tony. Sergeant Warner said, "You don't mind if we take Santa away for a while, do you?" Heather nodded and smiled to let him know that it was OK for him to go with the family.

She finished her lunch and paid her tab. When she walked downtown she saw Tony surrounded by a large crowd. She could see that most of these people were the families of the soldiers that served with Tony. They were having a hug-fest. Everyone took their turns in posing with Santa. She almost felt sorry for Tony since he was ambushed from all sides. But it seemed to her that he still had an endless supply of energy.

As it got closer to 5:00pm, Heather had her camera crew set up at the gazebo in the park. They spent about an hour filming Tony with the children. He was remarkable with the kids. He would not only ask the kids what they wanted for Christmas, but he would also ask them what they would do for their parents so they could have a wonderful Christmas, too.

Heather went back to her hotel room to write her story for her news channel. The raw video had already been sent to her station for editing. She was on the phone with the editors working on making the story flow. All sequences had to be in the proper order. Within a couple of hours, the editors had produced a segment that was great. She thought about how she would introduce the story and wrote down some notes. She had already filmed some "teasers" for her news station. These were short ads on what the story would be about. In one teaser she said, "Coming up on the ten o'clock news cast I will show you what is claimed to be the world's most perfect Santa." On another teaser she said, "No one has been able to capture the 'why' about this perfect Santa. But tonight I have an exclusive on why this man becomes the perfect Santa and how this sleepy town was able to help him work through his past."

Heather's story was scheduled to go live on Channel 21 News-Denver at 10:10pm that evening. Since Denver's time zone was one hour earlier than Blackwater's time zone, she would be live at 11:10pm in Oklahoma. She had her camera crew set up in front of the Santa Village in the middle of town. It was a school night so the town square was deserted except for a few town's people hanging around.

When she got her cue from the station in Denver, Heather went live.

"Heather Smith has been on assignment in Blackwater, Oklahoma this week," said the news anchor as he was segueing into her story. "I hear that you found the perfect Santa. In Oklahoma? Really?"

She responded on cue. "That's right. Blackwater, Oklahoma has been the home of the perfect Santa, so say the folks around here. I was sent on this assignment because our news director even heard of this Santa and wanted to know more about him. This story has a wonderful ending, but the beginning was not so wonderful. I call this story 'When Christmas Comes Home from the War.'"

At that moment the news station cut to the previously taped and edited content that her camera crew had captured. In the next five minutes she traced the story of Tony from the optimistic minister to the broken chaplain that returned from the war. For background impact Heather had taken photos of Tony and Georgia's wedding picture from Tony's house and pictures of Tony in formal uniform as well as the fatigues he wore as he shipped off to Viet Nam. Those pictures were hanging in museum in Blackwater. Heather beautifully wove the story of disappointment and depression that Tony witnessed and experienced for himself as he was in the middle of one of America's bloodiest wars. Then expertly, she told the story of what happened on the night of December 10, 1969. She told of how his patrol was ambushed. Tony was knocked unconscious. When he awoke, he was alone in the jungle. He happened across another patrol who had also been ambushed. She told of how Tony led the mission of five men to rescue another five men from the enemy. "That night, Chaplain Anthony R. Sanders went from being a minister to being a sniper," her voice-over explained.

Right after this a tape of Dr. Billings was played. She had returned to his office and had him re-explain why Tony's negative experience during the war may have been more traumatic that other soldier's experiences. The Dr. said, "Tony was trained, heavily trained as a minister and a chaplain. He was not like the other soldiers there. So when his world in which his greatest desire was to save souls collided with the world in which he took a life, the collision of the worlds was violent."

"That's may be why Tony's PTSD has stayed with him for almost fifty years," Heather explained in her voice-over as the tape showed the picture of Tony and nine other soldiers walking back into camp that night. The tape also showed the picture of Tony receiving the Medal of Honor from President Nixon less than a month after the December 10th horror.

The next part of the story showed how the town's people came together and planned a long overdue reunion with the soldiers that were with Tony that night. Heather was careful not to take any praise for the fact that she came up with the idea. She focused the story on how the whole town got together to produce the Hero Homecoming. She did mention Tim McAlester, Tony's best friend growing up, who gladly paid for all of the expenses incurred by the families of the soldiers to get to Blackwater on the anniversary date of that tragic night during the war.

The taped segment ended with showing shots of Tony bringing Christmas happiness to everyone he came across. Heather's voice-over told of how the perfect Santa was born out of idea that Tony felt he needed to do penance for what he did that night. But the hope was that the reunion would help him finally break out of the penance cycle and help Tony to be the Santa Claus because he wanted to be, bringing joy to the world. It was a beautiful way to end the story.

The news editor cut back to Heather live in Blackwater. "So today, like clockwork, former Army Chaplain Anthony R. Sanders donned his Santa suit and for the next few days becomes the perfect Santa. The whole town is hoping that the Hero Homecoming that they put on for him will help him come out of his depression and help him be just Tony, the happy and healthy man he was before the war. Of course, only time will tell. I will return to Blackwater in January to see how he is doing. This is Heather Smith, Channel 21 News-Denver."

The news cast cut back to the news anchor who thanked Heather for the heartwarming

Christmas story. In her earpiece she heard her boss, Randy Smith, tell her it was a wonderful story and he was proud of her.

Heather crashed in her hotel room that night. She had spent the last two weeks living out of a suitcase, going fast all day long every day, to get the story. She was understandably exhausted.

As she was getting dressed he next morning she turned on the TV just to have something to watch. She was surprised to see that Good Morning America, a morning news show on ABC, was rerunning her story. The celebrity cast was praising the story and commenting on how they are eager to see if the Hero Homecoming helped Chaplain Sanders in the long run.

She was so excited that she called Randy her boss. It was an hour earlier in Denver, but he was awake. "Did you see that my story was picked up by Good Morning America?" she said excitedly.

"Of course," Randy said. "Our switchboard lit up after your story. Everyone seemed to enjoy it. I got a call from the producer of GMA who asked if he could re-run the story. I see an Emmy in your future."

Heather was excited about the possibility of winning an award for her story. But that's not why she did the story. She started to panic a little thinking about the possibility of a flood of news reporters invading Blackwater to get their own story on Tony.

When she packed her things, she walked over the café for breakfast. Tina was there, as usual. "Well, there's the celebrity right now!" she bubbly exclaimed.

"You saw Good Morning America, didn't you," Heather replied.

"Yep," Tina said. "We had it going on our TV over there. There were only a few people here at the time. But they sure enjoyed it."

"That's great. But I'm worried about Tony," replied Heather with a concerned look on her face. "I'm afraid that there will be a lot of news people here in the next few days. I'm afraid that they will be harassing him for interviews."

"Oh don't worry about that," said Tina with a smile. "He's dealt with reporters before. He knows how to handle them. Remember when you first met him? Not exactly a welcoming conversationalist."

Heather thought back to the first time she met Tony. He told her "I don't like reporters!" He would be OK.

"And besides that," Tina continued, "if we have a bunch of extra people in town for the Christmas holiday, more money is brought in. I suppose I'll be very busy this year. And excited Christmas people give bigger tips."

Tina left to put Heather's order for breakfast in. She ordered her usual breakfast. In her mind Heather conceded that the influx of reporters and curious citizens would be a good thing for Blackwater. But she still wanted to talk to Tony and warn him of the possible bombardment of questions from reporters.

Heather finished her meal and walked around the down town area of Blackwater. It wasn't hard to find Tony. He was surrounded by shoppers and small children. When Tony saw her standing and watching, he went over to talk with her.

"Good morning, Heather," he said kindly. "You really caused a stir with your news story about me." Tony had not seen the story. He wasn't interested in watching news on TV. But he had already heard about it from his wife and the hundreds of people he had already seen that morning.

"Oh Tony, I'm sorry about all that," Heather apologized sheepishly.

"Sorry for what?" Tony asked.

"Well I'm afraid that there will be more reporters come to town to do their own story on you," she said. "I'm afraid they will distract you from being your jolly self this Christmas."

"Don't worry about me. I know how to handle reporters," he said as he gave Heather a wink. "I'll answer a couple of questions then shoo them away. I have Christmas cheer to spread."

With that, Tony excused himself and went back to the crowd that was waiting for him. Heather smiled. She knew he would be OK. And she was hoping deep in her heart that there would be a real change in Tony after the Hero Homecoming went off well.

Heather went back to the hotel to finish packing up her things. She checked out, got into her rental car, and headed to the airport in Tulsa. She had a fairly long wait at the airport for her flight. She decided to call her boss and see what else was going on.

"Hi Randy, it's me," Heather said. "Anything new about my story? Any other major outlets want to replay it?"

Randy was excited. And for a man who never really got excited about anything, Heather enjoyed hearing him talk. He told her about other news stations that wanted to run her story. "As soon as you get back her you need to run some promos and intros for those stations."

The intros included using the other station's name in the opening or the closing remarks. Like, "This is Heather Smith reporting for KMJE News in Omaha." When she arrived at her offices in Denver she spent the next several hours taping intros for other stations.

When she finally got home she tried to relax. But she put on her calendar that she wanted to return to Blackwater and do a follow up story on Tony. She put the note on Wednesday, January 15th. She was excited to see what happened after the Christmas season.

A NEW LIFE FOR AN OLD WAR HERO

Heather pulled into Blackwater about 10:00am. It had been just over a month since she was last in this beautiful sleepy town. She took the early flight from Denver to Tulsa. And since she missed breakfast, she headed to the café to get some good cooking.

Tina, the bubbly waitress, noticed Heather right away. "Hi Stranger! You just couldn't stay away from here, could you?"

"To be honest, I have missed you and Blackwater," Heather admitted. "It's good to be back."

"The usual?" Tina asked. She knew what Heather liked for breakfast. She poured a cup of coffee and ran off to the kitchen.

Heather scanned the café to see if Tony might be there. She was hopeful. But she was not surprised that he wasn't there. He usually came only for dinner.

When Tina came back with her breakfast, Heather asked, "Have you seen Tony lately? Is he OK?"

"Well, I still see him almost every afternoon around 4:15 or so," Tina answered. "He seems like his old self, you know, quiet, doesn't want to talk much."

A small pain developed in the pit of Heather's stomach. She was hoping that the Hero Homecoming changed Tony. The news from Tina was a bit discouraging.

"But Georgia says he's doing better," Tina continued. "She comes in every-once-in-a-while for coffee and a piece of pie."

That made Heather feel a little better about Tony. She finished her breakfast and headed over to

Tony's house. And, as usual, Georgia met her half-way up the walk and gave her a big hug.

"Welcome back home," Georgia said enthusiastically. "I knew you were going to come back and see how Tony was doing. Come on in!"

The ladies went into the house and sat down with some hot tea. "So, how's Tony been doing? Does he seem better?" Heather left the question broad and open-ended. She was hoping that Georgia would offer a lot of information.

"Well, to be honest," Georgia began, "he's changed quite a bit. I think what we did for him worked. He's not cured. But there are some bright spots every day."

"Does he still disappear into his apartment?" she asked. "I'm not trying to be nosey. Just trying to understand how he has changed, how he has improved."

Georgia began to blush. "Well, he doesn't live in the apartment any more. He sleeps in my bed. It sure is good to have a man to cuddle with at night."

"Wow!" Heather thought. "That's why she's blushing."

Then out loud she asked, "Is he here this morning?"

Georgia put a slight frown on her face. "No, he's at his counseling appointment with Dr. Billings. He had kind of a rough night last night. He was anxious about his session. He should be back any time now."

"A rough night?" Heather asked.

"He started talking about his counseling appointment," she explained. "And the more he talked about it and thought about, the more anxious he got. I made him some hot chocolate, you know, with real milk. Then I tried to get him to go to bed early. I hoped that he would go to sleep and stop worrying about the appointment. Up until last night things were going well."

Heather and Georgia talked for a long time. Heather made sure to ask about her feelings. She remembered that Georgia said, "He gets to tell his story all the time. But I don't get to tell my story."

Right at 12:00 noon, Tony walked in the door and said, "What's for lunch?" That was before he noticed that Heather was sitting with his wife. "Well hi, Miss Heather! Welcome back to Blackwater!" Heather stood to shake Tony's hand. But she received a big hug instead.

Tony looked exactly as she remembered. He wore frumpy clothes and a Denver Bronco cap and a scarf that didn't match the cap or the coat.

"Thank you," she responded. "I came to see how you were doing."

Tony thought for a moment. "I think things are going pretty well. Started sleeping with my wife again. Haven't felt the urge to yell at anyone lately. So, pretty well."

Heather smiled as she tried to figure out the next questions to ask. She looked at his cap and said, "You like the Denver Broncos, I see."

"Yep. Love Elway. But he hasn't done a good job of hiring a coach lately," Tony said. "I need to go up there and have a heart to heart with him. Straighten him out."

Elway referred to John Elway, former MVP quarterback for the Broncos. He is now the general manager whose job it is to hire the team's coaches.

The last few years the Broncos have gone through a few coaches. No one has been outstanding lately.

"Georgia says that you had kind of a rough night last night. Any special reason for that?" Heather tried to ask the question so that Tony would not get defensive.

"Yah, I was stressing over my appointment today," he answered. "Things have been going pretty good for me since you did that thing for me. I think I was stressing because my shrink was going to make me tell the story again. Wasn't looking forward to that."

"Well, how did it go?" she asked.

"Pretty good, I'd say," Tony answered. "I got to the part where, you know, I shot the guy. I cringed and closed my eyes. But I didn't yell at the shrink. That was a first."

Heather was surprised that Tony could talk about when he "shot the guy" without stopping or tearing up or yelling. That was a good sign.

Tony thought for a moment, then changed the subject. "I hear you got some award for your story about me."

"Well," she began, "I haven't received any awards. But I've been nominated for an Emmy and an OAB."

The Emmys are TV awards given out to, among other things, news services who do an outstanding job in reporting. The OAB awards are given by the Oklahoma Association of Broadcasters for outstanding reporting.

"There might be other awards," she continued, "but I'm not that excited about awards. And, I didn't do the story on you just to get awards. I really cared about you."

"I know you did," Tony said. "I'm glad you cared. I'm glad you helped me out."

Georgia got up to make lunch for Tony. She invited Heather to eat with them. She declined the food since she had just eaten her breakfast. But she did stay to talk with Tony and Georgia while they ate.

Heather was pleased to hear of Tony's improvements. She asked if she could get the both of them on video. She used her cell phone to capture their interview. Surprisingly, cell phones take good quality videos. Heather had used cell phone videos with other stories that she covered. She also asked Tony if it would be OK to contact Dr. Billings and interview him on video as well. Tony agreed and made the call to his shrink.

"Tell me about life after Santa Claus," Heather asked. "So, you didn't 'crawl back into the hole' as you described it to me. What else changed?

"It was the penance thing," Tony said. "I told you before Christmas that I wasn't thinking about the penance, you know, after that reunion you arranged. I enjoyed being Santa a whole lot better. And I don't think I thought about crawling back into the hole. Usually I did the Santa thing and worried about it ending. The closer I got to Christmas the more stressed I became. I told my shrink that very thing this morning. But that didn't happen this year."

"I am so glad that your life is a bit better now," she said. "I'm glad I had a little something to do with it."

"A little something?" Tony said as he raised his voice. "What you did was great! I still want to adopt you."

Tony and Heather and Georgia had a great lunch together, though Heather didn't eat anything. She left their house at 1:30 so she could get ready to meet with Dr. Billings at 2:00pm. Her head was swimming with questions. She wrote a few of them down but decided to rely on her memory when she was able to talk with him. Even the doctor seemed a bit happier. He had a big smile on his face as he welcomed Heather to his office.

"Come on in and have a seat, Miss Smith. Glad you're here," he said cheerfully.

"Thank you," Heather said. "I just came from Tony's house. He and Georgia seem to think that things are going better for Tony. Are you seeing the same thing?"

"Oh yes. Tony is talking differently. And at least for today, he is not as miserable when talked about the story." Dr. Billings explained again why it was important for Tony to repeat the story each time he came in. Retelling the story is one therapy that helps a person accept trauma in life, "And it helped me see the difference in vocal tone and body language as Tony talked. He seems to be handling his life better than before you came."

Heather smiled. The doctor went on. "Miss Smith, how did you come up with the idea of getting his old army buddies to have a reunion in Blackwater? I would like to know what went on in your mind."

"Well, I know that I'm not a mental health expert at all," she began. "But it seemed to me that Tony was stuck on the number ten. There were ten soldiers that came out of the jungle that night. But the mathematics weren't right. For him, it seems, ten living and safe soldiers did not erase the image of the one man he shot that night. So in my mind it seemed that if we could let him see that he was responsible for hundreds of living, loving and happy people, maybe the mathematics would encourage him to look away from the war instead of back at the war, back to that horrible day. I really didn't know if it was going to work. But I felt that I needed to try. Tony's friend Tim McAlester said he would pay anything. So I made the proposal and he went with it."

The doctor spoke up and said, "Well it was wonderful and it worked. In fact, I made a proposal to a couple of magazines in the mental health world and I would like to write an article about what happened. It won't be as crowd pleasing as your news story. My audience will be mental health professionals that expect a certain theoretical and philosophical language. I'm sure my readers will enjoy the article. But you might not."

Heather and Dr. Billings talked for a little while longer. She asked if he would explain a couple of things on video that she could include in her follow-up story. He agreed and eloquently spoke of how and why Tony changed as a result of the Homecoming he experienced. The doctor had a 3:00pm session. Heather left his office with a good feeling about the outlook for Tony's life.

Before she left Blackwater she drove over the Tim McAlester's office. She wanted to offer a heart-felt thank you to him for what he did.

"Hi Tim," she said excitedly. "I hope you know how wonderful you are for funding the Homecoming for Tony. I have seen a change in the way Tony looks at the world and how he looks back at the war. And I talked with Dr. Billings. He said he same things. If it weren't for you, none of this could have happened."

"Oh, no need to praise me," Tim said with a little embarrassment. "I wanted to do it and would do it again if it needed to be done."

"It must have cost quite a bit of money to get all those people to Blackwater," Heather said hoping that Tim might disclose how much he paid out for the Homecoming. Tim would not oblige her in revealing the cost. He was a business professional and he stayed professional as he talked about the Homecoming.

"To be honest," he said, "it didn't cost as much as I thought it would be. I almost feel guilty that I got a bargain funding the Homecoming. And I would like to keep the numbers to myself. My wife knows, but we're partners."

Heather told Tim about other good things that came out of the Homecoming. She told him about the awards for which she had been nominated. She told him about the article that Dr. Billings was writing and would submit to two magazines in his field of expertise.

"But Tony was the biggest beneficiary," she said and she brought the conversation back to the real reason everyone worked so hard. "Without your help Tony might not have ever come home from the war." She teared up a bit, gave Tim a big hug, and said her "good byes" to him.

She drove back to the airport in Tulsa. Her plan was to fly in, get some information and some video, and fly back home the same day. She caught the 5:30 flight to Denver and, because of the time change, she landed in Denver at 5:45.

She drove straight to her TV station. She had already sent the videos ahead of her arrival. When she got to her office she was able to help edit the videos and create her monologue that would accompany the videos.

About ten minutes after 10:00pm the news anchor introduced Heather and promoted her follow-up story of the Hero Homecoming.

"Heather, it's good to have you back. I understand that you have been working on a follow-up to the 'When Christmas Comes Home from the War' story."

"Yes, I just got back from Blackwater, Oklahoma where former Army Chaplain Anthony R. Sanders lives. He was still fighting Post Traumatic Stress Syndrome that came home with him from the Viet Nam War. I was sent to find the real story behind this war hero who helped rescue nine US soldiers on December 10, 1969. What I found was a man who was stuck, wallowing in grief over the one enemy soldier he killed. And he would not allow the thought of helping save the lives of US soldiers to erase the horror of killing one enemy soldier.

"The whole town of Blackwater got together and created the Hero Homecoming for Chaplain Sanders. Seven of the soldiers he helped rescue that night, plus all of their relatives gathered in Blackwater. The town wanted to help Chaplain Sanders see that there weren't just nine soldiers that benefited from his heroic rescue mission. He was able to see that hundreds of US citizens are alive and doing well because of what he did that night. I reported that the Hero Homecoming worked in helping change Chaplain Sanders. But I went back this week to see if those changes did in fact happen and if they produced lasting results."

The news stationed cut to the videos that Heather took of Tony's wife. She told the world that Tony was living in the house again. She blushed as she talked about being able to cuddle with him at night. Then the video from Tony himself was shown. Tony talked about how he didn't think much about the penance part of his actions. He was moved so much at the Hero Homecoming that his Santa duties were more fun than ever before. He also explained how he didn't yell and cry when he retold the story of December 10, 1969 to his psychologist. Tony's segment ended as he told the world, "I love this woman here" talking about Georgia his wife. "She has been so patient with me. I hope I can make it up to her."

"I was also able to interview Dr. Jeffrey Billings the VA psychologist who has been taking care of Chaplain Sanders for the past few years," Heather reported. The video of Dr. Billings was well done. He thanked Heather and all of the towns people of Blackwater for making the Homecoming a fantastic event. He told them that there would be more sessions coming up for Tony, but that he would slowly get back to the state of mind that he wants.

As Heather concluded her part of the news cast she cautioned everyone from thinking that the one big event was all that Tony needed to get back to where he wanted to be. "PTSD is a gripping disease and does not want to let go. It will still be a rough road ahead for Chaplain Sanders. But with the help of family and friends, he will get better. As for the perfect Santa, he told me he would continue to it every year. But now there is a lot more fun involved and he has a lot great feelings increase as he helps people enjoy the Christmas spirit."

Heather put her notes down and looked straight into the camera. She had a special ending for her special story. This is how she signed off the news cast that night.

"When Christmas comes home from the war, it's never like it was before. But with the help of a few hundred close friends, this war hero finally started leaving the war behind him, and returned to his home. And I am hoping that soon, in the very near future, I will be able to say 'And they all lived happily ever after.' This is Heather Smith reporting, Channel 21 News-Denver.

www.ingramcontent.com/pod-product-compliance
Lightning Source LLC
Chambersburg PA
CBHW032000240626
47153CB00003B/1063